A MAN, A GHOST

T. Seidenburg

LOUDHAILER BOOKS

Dedicated to
Madison Holleran

1

At dawn, per his usual routine, the president of our acclaimed media giant, *The Absolute Watch*, motioned to his personal staff clerk to draw his curtains, to whisk them aside so that he might be physically faced with his new day. The sun was peeking. The light bled onto the top corner of the wall in his bedroom, coincidentally adjacent to his office where, in mere moments, he would begin his regimen of a strong, black cup of coffee and pen his premature newsletters.

The chief clerk, relaying this gesture to his staff of minions, snapped at the two sullen-faced interns as they lashed the drapery to opposite ends.

Now wearing a mask full of glittering rays, the president proclaimed, "Ah! The sun is shining on me! This must be a sign of good faith from a world that needs me!"

However cheerful this man might appear to you at this very instant, his routine could teach you that he was, in fact, a man of the most morose character. Every course of action needed to fulfill his scheduled planner was stacked like a wall of bricks in front of him. Through his laborious efforts, he must—and I do not speak lightly here—assemble every facet of this empire brick by boring brick. Of course, he was a successful man! Success is only measured by others in the objective sense due to the appearance of one's achievements and possessions. Needless to say, he had very much. Keeping up this facade for himself was quite easy because he had been, over and over, building with the same materials for years—no matter how cheap or expensive, no matter the location in which he attained them.

Arnold Esche had been a young baron who inherited a fortune bequeathed to him by his late father, Alfred. This bold and good-standing man had always let Arnold know the consequence of sitting on one's hands.

"Arnold!" He remembered well the bellow of his enormous voice. "You must be active, son! Let no other take your place among the stars!"

This spoken edifice had never left Arnold's mind for but a millisecond. Like his father before him, he was a tall, imposing man of almost the exact same nature. The only discernible difference between them was the mannerisms to which they took on public opinion. Alfred was a bit of a recluse when it came to the actualization of another's tendencies, while Arnold took them strictly to heart. Therefore he had decided to merge his ambitions with that of his senior's lust for stardom. It was rumored that on the very first hour, in its infancy, he was to have reiterated to his initial partner, Andrew Allman, "The people! Without them, we are nothing!"

The Absolute Watch had been the brainchild of Arnold's for many a year, and only recently did it tempt him to build up a collection of alternative facts and begin to twist them in his favor. Oh no! Please do not think that this business was the result of him growing it from a rosebud! This transformation had taken place from a properly planted seed that abided alone to become a full-blown rose with its thorns fully grown and its red blush radiant. Located on a bustling outskirt of the prominent city of Downington, England, this outlet of information was a top contender in the inner workings of the urban environment.

Many prominent businessmen and businesswomen sought out its articles to assess the daily life of those to whom they would otherwise never encounter. It was overheard in the cozy cafés and small eateries:

"Arnold is a genius!"

"He understands us so well! Even without talking about us individuals in particular!"

"People are, indeed, the central muse from which we are to gain knowledge of ourselves!"

It was true. Mr. Arnold Esche had a keen eye for the most talented writers and the greatest social minds of the time. When he had personally scouted columnists, wined them with age-selected bottles, dined them, and offered them a large sum, they had almost no choice but to capitulate, and they truly would—considering their profession of personal, detached thought and output. This had gained him instant adulation. One writer, whom he had once kept on his personal staff, wrote a full article on the effects of democratic socialism on the public of Downington that had won him a literary prize for humanitarian effort. In a matter of mere months, this famed apogee of a business had soared into a new realm of legitimacy.

However, by the standards of Arnold's father, this was simply not enough! There were still other forms of competition out there for this man to trump, and he was not going to let a little stardust interfere with his ultimate position at the very pinnacle of universal acclaim.

So being the painstakingly driven man he was, he opted for a merger. Oh, do not for a second, one second, believe that Mr. Arnold Esche would even imagine liquidating his own personal stock! No, he had—at the expense of great personal risk—sought out a partnership in Downington. He made certain he was the beneficiary of 51 percent, with an innovative and ramped-up production factory. Its sole owner, Andrew Allman, had all the means to produce an astonishing amount of product. At the time these were flimsy aluminum cans and recycled-paper boxes, to which Arnold could not contain his excitement.

"We shall press millions! Millions of papers! Everyone within our borders shall feast their eyes on our ability to deliver our news, jam-packed with all types of intrigue, to anyone and everyone, willing or not yet knowing they are willing!"

At this very moment, Mr. Allman cringed at the thought of this expansion, but—it should now be clear to the reader—he did not have much of a choice in the matter. There was simply no more business floating his way, due to varied practices in production. Moreover, he just did not have the wit or stomach to delve into other areas that would make his factory prosperous.

At this very moment, the reader may be pondering what train of thought led Arnold Esche to select Mr. Allman to be his collaborator. Albeit Arnold being an astute, calculating man, he had possessed a burning desire for companionship. Not of that with another like-minded autocrat, but that of a prestigious individual of the objective kind. His years of schemes and plots had taken an empty toll on him, and he was longing to add a magnificent jewel to his crown, orb, and scepter.

Laboring arduously in the factory—of what was to become the new *The Absolute Watch* headquarters—upon Arnold's first arrival was our young and astounding Genevieve Allman. An adherent woman of about twenty, she was no stranger to hard work. Naturally radiant with a modest build, she boasted a well-shaped face covered by lengthy, reddish blond hair, with a rounded-off nose located ever so carefully in the center upon it.

And of course, Andrew Allman was all too willing to bring his wonderful daughter to light (!), hoping this would surely attract the attention of his honored guest. As he and Mr. Arnold Esche approached, an air of immediate attraction indeed arose!

At first glance—as any proper, aware person would— Genevieve was highly skeptical. However, being the sharp woman she most confidently was, she was able to play into the hands of this seemingly easily won figurehead. Her soft, inquiring facial expression most certainly influenced Arnold, and he too knew—all too well, may I add—that he was being swindled into choosing this facility to breed his future business endeavors.

Genevieve Allman was indeed a beautiful and forthcoming creature. However, much like Arnold himself, she was a woman of strict principle. She had been educated in the art of human likeness ever since childhood. Her mother, the late wife of Andrew, had died in childbirth—this was perhaps why our dear Mr. Allman was hesitant and void of risk! As a youth, she had not grown into herself quite as much as the other children, both physically and of prowess. She was beaten and teased to a degree of self-degradation. As Andrew was busy with his works, she was unattended and neglected for quite some time.

This was, of course, until she had made the acquaintance of a young man by the name of Robert Allagash. This boy, who had ever so accidentally been gerrymandered into the city of Downington by the mistake of a government official, was placed into a special classroom for the socially underprivileged youth along with our dear Ms. Allman. It should be noted that he was placed into this class because the incorrect action had been recovered by an even higher-ranking official, and this was the child's post until the error could be corrected.

As the curriculum of this class focused on the social construct of elementary learning, most of the lessons were done in pairs. Though you may believe it as a given fact, coincidentally their surnames had placed them at the top of the class list. For the first leg of term, personal introductions became the general lesson plan for our two youths. They exchanged names, physical attributes, and perhaps most important of all, conversation.

Robert was a boy of extremely high intelligence, and if it were not for his present situation, he would have been placed in his county's most prestigious school for gentlemen. Perhaps our Genevieve's fondest memory of her well-conceived comrade was a game he had played with her called "You and I."

"We are different!" he exclaimed. "You are a girl, and I am a boy."

"This I know to be true!" she giggled.

She was much perplexed at the simplicity of this activity, but she had let him finish on the grounds of her curiosity.

"We are different, you see, however we do have so much in common. We are both children. We both laugh, we play games, and we, as people, communicate with each other to get our points across."

"I . . ." Genevieve was thinking hard for a moment to respond, "I . . . I see we are very much alike as well!"

"But that is just the simple fact of it all!" he insinuated. "Which is more important for us? Our similarities that bind us or the things that divide us into separate identifications?"

A question that ran much too deep for children with such an unformidable experience!

About a fortnight after this rousing match of agnosticism, our Robert Allagash had been placed into his proper fraternity of the intelligentsia class of bourgeois society. Though he might have left Ms. Allman to wonder and wallow in her thoughts and dreams, she had always left these roundabout questions unanswered. This she did most purposefully until it could be answered at the proper moment.

Naturally, for accumulation of wealth and future prosperities, Genevieve did indeed accept a position as

Mr. Arnold Esche's personal secretary, when offered. This was the music of a thousand classical pieces to Arnold's ears. Now, Andrew Allman would no longer linger on the question of his daughter being taken care of financially—seeing as how Mr. Arnold Esche was the majority shareholder.

It may seem to the reader that this was a great deal of trust being put into a man with such capitalistic tendencies, but may I remind you that Arnold had been publicly well received with bursting universal acclaim in his industry, and Andrew was a man of simplicity and baseness.

The matter of signing the official documents took a fair amount of time as any transition of power would. Mr. Arnold Esche had a team of skillful lawyers at his disposal while Mr. Allman was forced to read over the papers of transactions alone. Genevieve had been with her father assisting in this process for many a day and night.

"Father," she appealed in an air of eager sincerity, "do you think it wise for only the two of us to be scanning this declaration alone? Needn't we an official man or woman of law to peruse these lines for error?"

"My dear, dear Genevieve! What choice have I? Very soon I won't have but a farthing!"

This was unfortunately, and most unbearably, true. Andrew was a man of gambling, drink, and vice. He had never saved a cent in his existence. At one interval of production, stemming from his various contracts, he had amassed a modest sum of wealth. He celebrated by frequenting the tavern and leaving the means of his operations to his juniors. He signed reckless deals that he could not fulfill in due time, which started costing him capital, labor, and respect. Then, at the climax of his downfall, his leading accountant had robbed him of a tremendous tranche that left him borrowing from various lenders. It is enough to make any man weep.

Perhaps worst of all, the man could not take the blame for himself! He was oblivious to the fact that he had made any decision that decreased his presence in the production realm. He was heard shouting by a worker in his warehouse, "Damn it all! I suppose business as usual has taken a turn for the worst!"

This assumption that his investments in time and material had simply vanished due to the competitive market and situation protruding from elsewhere might just be the most depressing aspect of them all. After consulting with former associates—most of whom had fallen victim to Andrew's selfish ways and decisions—Andrew Allman was, having already decided to sign these complicated papers before reading them attentively (!), ready to give his name by pen and sign his future, and the future of his beloved daughter, away to Mr. Arnold Esche.

Though this extensive agreement favored both of these gentlemen almost equally, the upper hand had clearly been given to Arnold Esche. Being aware of Andrew's habits, he was almost certain that he could, without much effort, push aside this man and reap the full spoils of their partnership.

A month or so later, Mr. Arnold Esche's hunch had come springing into life.

In the early hours, on a fine autumn morning, Arnold, similar to the beginning of our story, awoke in his chambers with the light shining upon him. As he dressed in his robes, he had begun work on an essay he wished to publish, with the topic focusing on experimental medicine from the Far East. He had selected the exact columnist he wished to craft this article and had scheduled a meeting with him for that very same day to discuss his knowledge on the matter.

"I know that this supposed method of acupuncture is absolutely ridiculous! However, imagine the look on the readers' faces! Foreign mysticism will surely grab their attention!"

It was just before six o'clock in the morning, and Arnold had realized that Andrew was rather late in his office the night before. As this was highly unusual, he thought it worthwhile to check up on the man's extra piece of work to see if he had merely been muddling around foolishly after dark to collect his thoughts, or if he had defiled his professional image by inviting over some less-than-reputable characters for a bit of exaltation.

As he rounded the corner to the bare, bulky wooden door with the name "Andrew Allman" stenciled upon its upper-right-hand corner, he pressed firmly on the door handle . . . and it was locked. Even more strange! Now began the task of beckoning the grounds department for the universal set of keys.

"Absolutely ridiculous!" Mr. Arnold Esche reacted with a bit of contempt. "I saw he was looking rather dreary and told the chap to go the hell home. And that was at noon yesterday!"

However, all that had been quite in vain. As the representative of the grounds crew came to open the wooden barrier, utter horror and shock had now been realized by the party of intruders. Upon his chair, leaning ever so far backward on the brink of snapping the seat in two, lay Andrew Allman almost flat, with his heels upon his desk, mouth wide opened with an empty bottle of brandy beside his left hand, now hanging motionlessly above it.

"Dear god! The imbecile!" Arnold shouted, showing not grief but lashing out at Andrew Allman's negligence.

As a heavy drinker, Andrew had lately taken to hard alcohol to soothe his woes. He had asphyxiated on his own vomit. Simply a poor way to go. No doubt he had been trying to get comfortable in his drunken stupor, but lying flat on his back, he was subject to his own sick. In their agreement of terms for the establishment, the ones which Andrew had so hastily looked over virtually alone, all his shares were to be given to Mr. Arnold Esche in the event of such a tragedy.

The news of her father's death came as almost no surprise to the oft-injured girl who had watched him ever so closely as a youth. Genevieve had sobbed for him only in pity. For now, he had left her quite alone in a world where she had to nominally fend for herself. Mr. Arnold Esche, not pleased but satisfied in the usurpation of Mr. Allman's shares, was willing to pay for the burial with his own personal funds.

It was a bleak and uncomfortable procession. He promised nothing more to himself than to fund a pauper's grave. The lack of attendees made the process unfailingly lonely. He was laid to rest on a plot of grassless dirt selected by Mr. Esche in the cheapest and most ragged part of Downington, where criminals and those who were too poor to afford a headstone were dumped by the means of funds from ecclesiastical tithings. The eulogy was quick, almost insincere, and there was no luncheon to celebrate the life of someone who might have been otherwise accomplished.

Standing over her father's forgone flesh and bones, Genevieve Allman wept in silence. A broad hand came across her shoulders. It was, of course, her haughty boss and the benefactor of her father's insignificant fruits of labor, Mr. Arnold Esche.

"My dear," he croaked, having been silent throughout the service. "I mourn your father's passing although you must admit he was the judge, jury, and hangman of his life!"

A most uncomfortable and odd thing to say given the circumstances—though she had known it for certain to be true. At this damning statement, Arnold turned to leave her in peace for a moment. But just as he was about to enter his carriage, he turned around to shout to her, "And now it is but you and I!"

Now that the whole of *The Absolute Watch* rested in the hands of its initial idealist, the full potential of the paper could be realized by Arnold Esche's vision. It was the beginning of a new fiscal year, and some staunch changes would now be taken into effect.

First order of business for Arnold would be to fire all of Andrew Allman's former employees who, he claimed, were not in tune with the revolution that would be taking place. Most of the gentlemen, in the time of Andrew's campaigns, were old fogies and fops that stood around and merely pushed buttons for the sake of making a dollar. They were not so much concerned with production as they were with making sure their ties were on straight and that their shoes were polished immediately after they had been scuffed. At the mention of their "receiving the ax," not one had fought for his employment.

"It seems as though we have died with the old fool as well!" one shift manager snapped.

"A great travesty! Nonetheless, there is always some other work elsewhere!" a canning line supervisor chimed in optimistically.

This group of old-fashioned men was resigned to the idea that this was just not their cup of tea any longer. They had no stomach for a fight that would surely have ruined their reputations among their inferiors—and the troubling whack it would be on their wallets as well.

This left around 15 percent of Andrew Allman's force at will, including Genevieve. They were all to be foot soldiers in this newfound warfare. Aside from Genevieve Allman, they were all laborers of the simple sort. However, what they lacked in brainpower, they most certainly made up for in knowledge of the necessary machinery. All were handymen capable of fixing these vast printing machines and assuring their running like clockwork. This was the only thing Arnold asked of them, and he would be sure to keep it that way. As for his new hires, the management team and liaisons of press, he searched low and high for the sharpest and most sincere minds of the coming age.

His first hire, Mr. Archibald Cunnings, was chosen to be the head director of his storyboard and vice president of *The Absolute Watch*. Archibald Cunnings had a graduate degree at the top university in Downington, with honors in journalism and human affairs. He was a short, bald, and round little man with even rounder spectacles. He had traveled to five continents on the expense of the university to study all walks of human life. Most notably, he traveled to Africa to study the indigenous tribes that had not yet contacted the outside world. Although he was a brilliant scholar, he was a bit of a yellow coward. Arnold knew he would bend the knee to him when asked, so that he made a stupendous second-in-command.

His next hire was a man of French descent. Pierre Libois—a tall, thin, and curling mustached man—had studied the daily procedures of factories all over industrial France while visiting family members and had only been back in Downington a short time for pleasure when he had heard about the great Arnold Esche and his information storm. Naturally, seeking the most efficient means to his personal wealth, he had sought him out and proposed to be his production manager. Enthralled with his enthusiasm and prior working experience with those of a proletariat background, Arnold Esche agreed to it being a stellar fit.

Last, and perhaps the most undervalued and best hire Arnold could have hoped for, was Dr. Erich Eicher—a man of German heritage who came from a patriarchal line of doctors and scientists. A psychologist by profession, he had been at a standstill in his own undertakings due to his failing personal efforts. He had worked as his own practitioner for quite some time; however, he had grown to become lost in his own meanderings. The doctor had matted brown hair, on top of his head and on his face, and possessed a slightly overbearing build. Arnold Esche had previously been a one-appointment patient of the doctor, and so he knew how he could tap into the feelings and beliefs of others so that they might truly reveal the passions of their deepest desires. Mr. Arnold Esche would use this tactic for his journalists to paint magnificent pictures of their subjects.

With this fantastic group of established scholars, Arnold Esche was sure he had absolutely nothing to lose, granting him unlimited freedom. They had come at a great price; however, he was almost certain that they could piece together a mosaic of wonder that thousands of people would continue to read daily. No doubt arose in the progress of his internal dialogue, and he was proven to be right many times over.

Indeed, success lay ever so easily on the doorstep of the front office of *The Absolute Watch*; however, the longer it lay, the feebler it became. Arnold's insatiable hunger would not be satisfied until he had a worldly article on which he could prove to be the ultimate provider of information.

On a damp, blustery morning in late fall, Arnold awoke with another grand idea. He had immediately skipped his morning coffee to write to his heads of staff that he would like to arrange a meeting with them in regard to another phenomenal project of his undertaking. This arousal of thought in his head had been quite a long time coming. Arnold knew the actions and intentions of others very well, but he had realized it had not come so deep as to have been perfectly true. He wanted to test and break the barrier of the human insight to form an "otherworldly" understanding of it. This became his obsession. He would send his colleagues on their separate ways to determine who, in their rightful studies, could catch, so to speak, this enigma of perplexity.

"I am a genius!" he muttered, almost inebriated by this wave of self-praise.

So it was that his team gathered that very afternoon. He burst into the conference area, posing a puffed chest and letting out a long breath of obvious intent.

2

Gathered around a long, rectangular table of oak, the three senior members of Arnold's newspaper ranks sat with anxious expectations. He had entered so robustly, and they had all glanced around to note each other's candid expressions. Sitting at the head of the consultation, he laid both hands down flat on their palms and orated what might have been his greatest speech to date.

"My dear and faithful comrades! It has not only been a pleasure but an honor to have worked with you these past few weeks. All seven days and hours of the week, we have strived to unveil to the public our piece of mind—as well as our piece of heart—that we so willingly bleed onto the pages of our journals. But I have yet to ask the most of you! It has come to my fervent attention that none of you are so competitively nor comparatively much more apt than one another. Your skill sets, in their own way, have challenged the very grounds to which writing has its standards set upon.

"Archibald Cunnings. Your plethora of ideas and understanding of what the reader would be intrigued in has undoubtedly helped to properly organize and sell more papers than what has ever been managed before. Our international subjects have been given new light in the face of your brokering with their governments. This is invaluable!

"Pierre Libois. Your undertaking of the production division has greatly increased our economic standpoint. Our costs have never been so ruthlessly efficient, and our materials have never had the quality that you are able to provide us with!

"Last, and certainly not the least, Dr. Erich Eicher. Your psychological analysis of the interviewee, before and after they have given their piece, has gifted the reader with more perspective than they could have dreamed of. Readers are not just getting a piece of scripture, but they are receiving a look into that person's experiences and intentions!

"Together, gentlemen, we have created a brand-new level of humanistic media. We have grouped words and ideas together to establish a living, breathing oracle. With these articles and columns, we have given new life to the population that exists around us.

"Perhaps you wonder why I have asked you all to meet for such a powwow. To praise you. But of course! However, there is an unmistakable task at hand. I am growing old, you see. I have no heir, no son, and no family. I do not wish to publicize my work, and I need one of you three to take the reins of *The Absolute Watch* so that I may retire with peace of mind."

The three members of the board were absolutely stunned. How could this man trust them when he had only just brought them to hire mere months ago? Many questions occupied their minds, but they had not but another few seconds to process what they had just heard.

"So this is my ultimate proposition. Each of you, immensely learned in different facets of social, psychological, and mystic humanism, will write for me a report on any topic regarding an individual or group of people anywhere in the world. You may write about their personality. You may observe closely their environment. But overall, this should be your own masterpiece. There are essentially no guidelines whatsoever."

At the very moment that he stopped pronouncing the last word of his finale, Genevieve broke into the room in hysterics.

"You monster! How dare you speak of the future of this business without including me in it?"

Arnold was not even taken aback. He simply called for the staff clerk to whisk her out of the room as if no words had even been spoken from her mouth.

"I will speak with you later," he spoke with coolness and calm.

Genevieve proceeded to be led unwillingly out of the room, flailing her limbs and attempting freedom.

"I apologize for our brief interruption. Now, do tell me, what are all of your initial impressions on the matter?"

Excited as he was in revealing his grand scheme, Mr. Arnold Esche understood that his senior staff was already quite busy with their own personal business matters. Could they truly imagine that he would have them halt their numerous goings-on to start a brand-new exposition? This would have to come to be accepted by the entire party present.

"But, sir, what of the current editions of the paper?" A concerned tone crept from Archibald Cunnings's lips.

"Ah! To hell with it. These readers have gotten the best material anyone could have hoped for in ages. What's the off chance they would ever stop reading? It would take years for them to turn us away . . ."

"But is that not just the point?" interrupted Pierre Libois.

"The . . . ? Well, I am almost certain these plebeians would continue to read our news even if I were to divert their attention astray for some time."

Arnold Esche had visited the thought as he had plotted this stupendous idea. What could be used to fill the pages of the newsletter while his team was busy amassing information of the most genuine kind?

"I suppose we could let the journalists handle our undertakings for a while—that is, with my supervision of course!"

There was an uneasy, unwilling feeling among those present at the meeting instantaneously. Mr. Cunnings, Mr. Libois, and Dr. Eicher were equally a bit unsettled. They trusted their superior, not unreasonably, in matters of organization and planning. But all three knew all too well that he would only bring about information that the citizens of *The Absolute Watch* would want to hear and not what they earnestly wished to know. Mr. Esche sensed that he was being doubted, so he immediately attempted to regain their confidence.

"Please do not think that I am to write the material myself! I promise you, gentlemen, for the sake of your own pay grade, that I shall hire better writers than were on our paper before!"

Yet still the faces of the three in front of him were bleak. Not to confirm their convictions, Arnold took a long draw of breath, attempting to calm his inner misgivings.

"Perhaps you all think that the pages are to turn yellow if I become the sole influence of our establishment?"

Indeed, this was the collective consensus. The integrity of *The Absolute Watch* was at stake, and not a single soul there, perhaps aside from Mr. Esche, wished it harm. However, if Arnold, in fact, broke bread with himself, that would be its ultimate demise.

Rising from his position on the left side of the table, Dr. Erich Eicher stood, not imposing but certainly not backing down, and spoke plainly and clearly on the situation, "Mr. Esche, the truth is something, we, my colleagues and I, take most seriously. The value of this virtue not only propels our reputation but the course of the events of the whole world. One man cannot simply be chosen to formulate conclusions alone, let alone ones that cater to his every whim, for he sometimes sees only what he wants to. I understand you are not alone here in this business, but your position of power also affects the opinions of others so that they may only say what you would like to hear. If you feed into their 'free speech' in this manner, they will surely whisper their own desires to you, and you will grant them these wishes based on your 'knowledge' of their initial propositions." Stunned, and sure that this would throw Arnold Esche into a frenzy, Mr. Cunnings sank deep into his chair.

Arnold collected his thoughts for a moment and, mirroring the doctor, rose to his feet as well, penetrated the doctor's eyes with his own, and vowed, "I could shoot someone in the middle of our town square and would not lose a single reader over it."

So it was! This was the irrevocable, final decision. An immovable force that could not be bothered with reason. Understanding the gravity of the situation, Dr.

Eicher had simply retaken his place without another word. How empty of a sentiment it must have been for the doctor to experience to hear such damning blasphemy. Alas, this was what had happened, and unmistakably, this was the obstacle that would have to be worked around.

Arnold put on a better-tempered face and thanked his advisers for meeting with him on such short notice. His hubris allowed him to become unaware of the opinions around him, and he was most certain that he had become the victor among such preposterous agitators!

As he left the conference area, a brief silence fell among those still seated in their black leather chairs. They were all imagining what it would be like to leave their posts in the palms of such an oblivious man.

"Perhaps we should stage a meeting among ourselves at this very moment?" Dr. Eicher would not simply capitulate immediately to Mr. Esche's plan.

Mr. Cunnings and Mr. Libois certainly knew he would be eager to add to their assumptions.

"You understand my position very clearly, I suppose?" Mr. Cunnings led with obvious intent.

"But, Archibald, you cannot ultimately believe that you should stay quiet about these misgivings? Think of the outcome. The pride that is attached to your doing right. The very reason you signed up for this job!" spoke the doctor, attempting to introduce reasoning.

"I let all of those things go straight to the heavens, my dear friend!"

Erich Eicher concluded beforehand this would be Archibald's stance on the matter.

"When I had been approached for this position, I made it my duty to go by Arnold's word. Not to question, not to advise upon, not to even mislead his exceptional, yet unorthodox, requests."

Archibald Cunnings was no fool and knew that all could be lost in an instant, but his own scholarly merit could not overthrow his grounded philosophy. He could very well find other employment in his professional field elsewhere—this just happened to be his best fit for the time being.

"Furthermore, I do wish you would cease meddling in Arnold's affairs! I understand your intentions, however I will not let you stand in the way of the man that writes your checks. Do you wish to have such great influence? If this is so, you might as well foster your own agenda and leave Mr. Libois and myself out of it!" Confident in his response, Mr. Cunnings brushed the argument aside and stepped through the French-made doors to return his attention to his daily schedule.

This left Dr. Erich Eicher and Mr. Pierre Libois glancing curiously at each other from across the conference table. They had not been familiar with each other even as associates at the newspaper, and this would be their very first private discussion.

"Please, Mr. Libois, enlighten me. What do you make of Mr. Esche's request?" In his first attempt to draw him from his reservations, Dr. Eicher was successful.

"I would like to think you are correct in your advancement of thought, Doctor, but as it has played out many times over, we both know that Arnold will apprehend what he desires. So perhaps we should just let him have it. I assure you that the precautionary steps he intends to take will soften the blow of his progressiveness."

Dr. Eicher was not sure that he understood exactly what Mr. Libois intended to relay. "But why leave it to chance? What could possibly be examined any further? We should, incontrovertibly, force him to be open-minded."

"But what do you, Doctor, intend to gain from his optimism? Why should you be spearheading his direction?" Mr. Libois had even more to say—certainly more than Dr. Eicher would have thought. "If wolves took their advice from sheep, they would lose their natural lust for blood! This is the very nature of their being. So let them be. For even if the wolf doth pray on the sheep, the sheep, in turn, becomes an actor on the stage of its surroundings. It acts on its own tried methods, so that it may even wear the skin of the wolf to disguise itself! Only then will it truly participate in the hierarchy of wildlife."

Dr. Eicher was perplexed at Mr. Libois's comparison of humans to animals. Why even attempt to place human value in bestial form?

"That is a most frivolous depiction of the situation! A mental consciousness does not exist for them as it is with us. I pity your poor taste in the lack of divergence of *Homo erectus*."

"For this lack of understanding, you shall surely fail to obtain Mr. Esche's bequest!" Mr. Libois was utterly bold in his speech. "Please keep in mind, Doctor, that the burden of high consciousness is a large cross to bear. If you let it, it shall break your back. If you leave it fully attended to, it will be the result of a child that will never leave its mother. The lamb that knows not how to defend itself will surely be prone to the consumption of the wolf."

Noticing that he had spoken with a bit of a forked tongue, Pierre stood mechanically and showed himself out of the room.

Dr. Eicher now remained in his place for a quarter of an hour, pondering what had been said. Why had Mr. Libois been so duplicitous in his language? Erich concluded that this must have been a nervous incident, for he obviously did not know this man so well. He concluded that Pierre was simply anxious about the monumental assignment, and because he was not as skilled in penmanship and literature as he and Mr. Cunnings, he felt a bit overwhelmed and void of such talents.

Within the four walls adjacent to the conference area, Arnold Esche had been vexed by a separate meeting—which he arranged quite regrettably. He had called Genevieve Allman into his office to ask her what exactly she planned to do to apologize for rudely interrupting his formal gathering moments ago. He was certain he knew why she had purposely become a thorn in his side, but he was now determined to prove it to her.

At first, he spoke softly, so as to coerce her into a confession of wrongdoing. "My dear, please, do explain your frustrations with me."

Expecting this attempt at a soft, entry-level coo, she retorted, "You understand that I view your activities every day, and you continually mock me by not including me in the economic long run!"

"Genevieve, you have a permanent place on my staff! What more could you possibly think that you deserve? Your father . . ."

"Do not bring him into this! I am nothing like that man!"

"But you are his offspring. There is no question about that." Now came the iron resolution of a practical businessman. "I am not disallowing you the chance to become a benefactor because of your family ties, I am preventing it because you are female."

The words seared like molten metal upon the ears of a refusal to be defeated. At the mention of her sex, she became unrelentingly hostile.

"You swine! You overexaggerating misogynist. I see the way you look at me. Those eyes glaring every single chance you get. You think I am wrong in my accusations, but I know the powers you possess!" A reddening of her face sustained.

"Genevieve, although the allegations you place upon me are quite true, I have never once attempted to make an advance. I wouldn't dream of it! I understand the relationship between us, and I would never betray that understanding." Arnold Esche was indeed very much convinced. "What you, on the other hand, must understand is that it simply is not good for business. It is not what I am like, but it is what they are like. My partners, my advisers, it is them I cannot control. I am only protecting you from that which you have no influence over."

"I do not need protection!" The state of her emotions had rightfully swelled. "Why is it that you still see me as a child? Not only infancy but inferiority as well! What difference does it make that I am female?" She was at a complete loss of conversation, so she blurted it out into unobstructed objectivity.

"It makes all the difference in the world, I am afraid." Arnold Esche drove the dagger home for his proceeding conformation. "We are much alike, Genevieve. You possess ambition, fierce determination, and resourcefulness. However, we are different simply because you are a woman and I am a man. It is not something that can be changed."

"Damn it all! I've heard this before! How could you be so obtuse? I am through with this conversation! Goodbye for today, sir."

With great emphasis on the formal declaration, and of her impending absence, she vigorously closed his office door behind her.

So it was that Arnold had a brief passing to brush the whole of the incident off before returning to his duties.

Poor Genevieve, he thought. *It seems that recognizing simplicity is not in her repertoire.*

Mr. Esche graced the floor of his operation and asked a staff clerk to perform Ms. Allman's engagements for the rest of the workday.

Later that evening, when all the bustle of this workday was through, Dr. Eicher gathered his personal belongings and a few extra pieces of work. He was in the process of snapping shut the lock on his briefcase when he heard a rapping on the door of his office.

"Please, do enter."

The figure of Pierre Libois stepped through the threshold of its frame. Holding one hand in the other, he appeared to be a smidgen bothered.

"To what do I owe this pleasure?"

"My dear doctor, I had been considering that the weight of my words was much too heavy this afternoon, and I would like to explain myself." Mr. Libois was grasping for the doctor to lend an ear.

"Proceed, please."

What Pierre Libois exerted next was, unbeknownst to him, vaguely similar to their first exchange.

"The comparison and contraction of the wolf and the sheep was a result of myself playing Virgil! I was simply fooling around with the idea of the republican Rome for our little project, and I was warping his words around to try to bring out his true essence along with yours as well. I am fully aware you cannot be riddled so easily in your standpoint, and I admit, I tried to shake it from you. Do not let me mislead you in the slightest. It was a cunning thing to do, and I do apologize, for it was most egregious."

The sincerity was noted by the doctor. "It was indeed deceitful, however I do believe it is due to your nerves. This is, to scale, a far reach for a man of production."

"My sentiments exactly! I spoke to Arnold just after our gathering, and he agrees that this will inevitably test my measure of wits. Therefore, I am being overtly competitive."

"Just be sure that the competition remains healthy, and you will not suffer the burden of your conscience."

"Oh ho, Doctor! I now see the extensiveness of your genius. You are much cleverer than I. You are a tree rooted on the highest of hills. You see all from afar."

Flattered but even more nervous for him than ever, Dr. Eicher petitioned for Mr. Libois to accept his credence.

"Let not this objective change you. Nothing has changed between you, me, and the circumstances surrounding the business. We are to race chariots against one another, but that does not call for running myself and Mr. Cunnings off the proverbial track."

"Thank you for your counsel, Doctor. I shall continue to keep a straight head regarding my research."

Turning his back to make way for the exit, he turned, once more, to face the doctor—his body was already halfway around the corner of the entry point.

"Doctor, I have one more confession to make." Mr. Libois doubled his motions back into the office. "Arnold— Mr. Esche, I mean—I don't believe I enjoy his company very much."

This resonated with the doctor. "Mr. Esche is a man worthy of some admiration, it is true, but I don't believe he shares a connection with others that appears to be genuine."

"I could not have articulated it better myself. I am exalted that you feel the same!" Those last few words were thrown into existence.

A firm handshake followed, and Pierre Libois showed himself out of Erich Eicher's office once more.

These minute exchanges between these two men were continuing to develop into a nuisance to Dr. Eicher; however, this was his internal reservation whenever he managed to break into the playing field of a potential patient's misfortunes. He had a very difficult time providing helpful advice most likely because he could never be able to take it himself when needed. He was tired from the day's proceedings, but this reminded him about his own trials and tribulations—one that currently awaited him as he hurried from the fortress of Arnold Esche and into the consuming darkness that approached with nightfall.

Best not to blow a fuse until it is a necessity.

This was his creed, for he knew the fate of his overexerted propulsions. He gradually pushed the ensuing bad weather from his mind and headed for the taxi which was accompanied by a personal valet.

Much later in the evening, surrounded by ignited candle trees scattered about, Arnold Esche was pouring two glasses of single-malt whiskey into crystal-clear highball glasses. This had been a running tradition in the weaning months of the Gregorian calendar year, and Arnold, an occasional partaker in drink, felt that it was appropriate to indulge in two or three measures. He saw fit to extinguish a dozen or so of the waxy figures in his office so he could glance out of the panes of glass and into the surrounding landscape omitting the glare that many lit wicks would produce. He held his potion in hand and began adding perfect, square cubes of ice. He turned to survey what lay beyond the gates of *The Absolute Watch* and had only a moment to wonder about the fruitful months ahead when the doorway was drawn open, creaking ever so slowly and longingly until Arnold had spotted the reflection of light in Archibald Cunnings's spectacles.

"Ah, Archibald, bless you for staying until this hour at my request."

"Certainly, sir."

Archibald coughed, a bit annoyed as he did not believe Mr. Esche regarded him as busy in his after-hours affairs. This, on the contrary, was a discussion between confidants.

Arnold began to pace toward Archibald Cunnings and carefully placed his hand upon his shoulder, looking him straight into his pupils.

"Archibald, my loyal, trusted friend"—*friend* being used condescendingly—"this editorial I have commissioned, it is all a sham."

Archibald Cunnings knew not what to make of this confession. Mr. Esche eagerly waited on him to reply, but Archibald Cunnings's face became serious and judgmental.

"Yes, I am afraid that I have already elected a successor myself!"

Obviously not as enthusiastic, Archibald Cunnings bowed and swiveled to make his exit when Arnold Esche clamored at his arm and turned him back around to face the latter.

"It is you, my good sir! You are the one to take on this colossal success!"

Not entirely certain how to proceed, Archibald Cunnings remained silent.

"Listen, I cannot be certain the paper will be run to my liking if Mr. Libois or Dr. Eicher heads its committee. I am to leave specific instructions for you because I know you will heed my word. I ask just one favor of you—one favor only." Arnold was now at the point of the resolution. "Archibald Cunnings, by duty and duty alone, I require you to apprehend an item abroad. It is located in the far reaches of Siberia. Of course, I cannot reveal the specifics, but it lies in a small bronze box. It is essential for you to obtain it, for it is most important for your ascent to becoming chief owner and operator."

Dumbfounded, Mr. Cunnings had finally gathered his thoughts to proclaim, "*Why* is certainly the most obvious question! But you did make it clear this question was not to be asked. If you are quite sure of it, sir, then it shall be completed."

"Exactly the conclusion I hoped you would come to indeed!" Mr. Esche gave him a handshake of approval, and then, swooping his hand down to grab the other glass of liquor, he prompted a toast. "To good fortune!"

The men both downed their glasses.

"If I must be curious about one thing, Mr. Esche, why will you continue to amuse our other two participants with their research?"

A valid type of question that was allowed by Arnold Esche.

"Let us leave it at the honing of their journalistic skills and style. We both understand, I am sure, that Mr. Libois and Dr. Eicher are not as well learned in the genuine affairs of others as we may be inclined to believe. I take it that both of them will work effortlessly to try and claim the paper for their own. Preoccupation is a catalyst for ignorance. If the cliché of not knowing truly is beneficial to a man, then they will have almost no trouble at all in their endeavors. Now the hour is approaching the morrow. Please travel to your abode and get some rest."

At Archibald Cunnings's dismissal, the unspoken confirmation of utmost secrecy was noted by both men. Archibald Cunnings strode off and down the stairwell where his valet awaited.

3

Dr. Eicher awoke in his chambers at home, contemplating the conversations he had engaged in with Mr. Libois, and it struck him that he was beginning to question his own motives in the wake of Mr. Esche's newfound arrangements. Realizing he was covered in perspiration, it had come to light. He had dreamed through the night that he was his own double, a scheduled patient, while conducting a psychological examination. This occurred to him always in his mind very much awake, but it seemed that in one's dreams, there were peculiar differences that one wished to control—a clear desire for it to reach unattainable perfection.

The first Erich Eicher sat in a wooden chair of oak; the second was lying down on a ruby-red sewn chaise longue complete with smooth, round buttons. He had supplied himself with sedative medication, one that would knock him out indefinitely. He began to ask himself reservations about his inner monologue.

"And what do you believe is the true course of human nature?"

Since this was his own formulated inquiry, he surmised, "To act staunchly conservative but think universally liberal!"

The first doctor was dressed in black robes, and the second doctor, on the sofa sporting white, merely chuckled at his response.

"My dear boy, it is quite the opposite of what you think! Your preconscious is controlling your suppositions. I, acting on behalf of what you know better, tell you that most are unconscious in their mental processing. How else would they become so physically able?"

At once they stood and exchanged robes, swapping positions seamlessly.

The next question now put into play by the previous patient was, "Are they only so able because they are so absent of their unconscious? Why then do we believe that we are the only ones conscious of such unconsciousness? Surely, there are others who formulate ideas the same!"

Sitting up hastily and pointing a firm index finger, his counterpart continued, "Ah, but asking this, contrary to my answer, would only expose your ego. For sputtering your ideal of a population that works harmoniously together is only a view from your brain and not your eyes!"

Both men simpered.

"Then I suppose you should continue wearing these dark dressings!"

"No, I shall not make another swap, this is the form of what we truly are! You wish to act without a preconceived notion, and I will have none of it! That is madness."

"I only wish to think not so much is all . . ."

Without notice, they switched back to their original linens.

"Let me enlighten you."

Now both doctors were upright on their respective furniture together.

"Sometimes perversions must be brought to light. In ensuring this, one may have to act liberally to wring out the disgustingness in another. It is not something that you can guess from their neurons but that you must observe in plain sight."

"I suppose, but what if you really could see their concealed beast? What then?"

"Then we would not have the problems we suffer from in this world. It is true that one may estimate the level of wickedness in another, but because part of it is kept within, we may never know their intentions until they play them out on the world stage. Therefore, we should not act until acted upon."

With this last evidence of his own circular statements, the medicine he took began to blur his vision.

"Good night, Doctor."

This was where the physical Dr. Eicher had been left to complete his dream cycle.

He lay on his back for over an hour. Much like his otherworldly apparition, he began, consciously, daydreaming of his point of view from his mattress.

I understand I am a fool and know nothing, but does that not mean I should not have a strong opinion? Certainly not. But to act out that opinion? Too liberal. It matters not that other people place judgment upon what you do, but you are a sustained character to only let them see what you wish!

Satisfied by his conclusion, Dr. Eicher rose from his resting place. It was almost ten o'clock in the morning, and the doctor had been expecting a planned visit.

A clanging bell was rung around noon, and Dr. Eicher raced to his door with the presumption that it was his long-awaited visitor, but he was most disappointed when Mr. Cunnings was rooted to his stoop, looking up at him with a nervous air, much like that of Mr. Libois at yesterday's end. The doctor motioned him inside, stepping away from the entrance so that Archibald could waddle through.

Removing a green bowler hat, Mr. Cunnings let out a long sigh and began to voice his concerns.

"Erich, for Mr. Esche's stake, I am going to Russia to study the legacy of the Romanovs. The Czarist dynasty has been of particular interest to him, so I believe this analysis will claim his prize."

Being as cold as it was in the weather outside, Archibald Cunnings was shivering to his core, and his teeth were chattering. This muffled a few of his words.

Dr. Eicher spoke, "You should be lucky to be traveling in a heated compartment. If that weren't the case, I dare say I don't think you would survive."

Giving the doctor a low-hearted smile, Archibald dug deep into his coat pocket and handed the former a creased and worn paper envelope, tied with a matching paper string. It was sealed with a uniform crest.

"And what is this?" Dr. Eicher inquired.

"Erich, please do not question my actions."

This was, perhaps, the first time Dr. Eicher had even seen Mr. Cunnings take control of a conversation before. The doctor remained silent and waited for Mr. Cunnings to proceed.

"This will be a long and perilous journey. That I am very much aware of. I do not speak lightly in saying this to you. But please, if anything should happen to my physical being, take this letter and present it to the Board of Governors of The Commerce and Wealth of England." This seemed of paramount importance.

"Why need I bring it to them? As an official member of a prominent business, you should be able to get them to speak on whatever issue it is that you would like to present."

"The timing is simply not right." Mr. Cunnings was looking dreadfully tired at this point. "Please, I beg of you.

This is my only request. Aye, it is a simple task, but do not forget it nonetheless."

Without a formal farewell, he flipped his hat back onto his head, and with his hands placed in his underarms, he battled back the wind to get to his carriage.

Left alone in the foyer, aside from picking apart his own aura, Dr. Eicher now focused on Mr. Cunnings's recent encounter. As a man of little risk, so it seemed to the doctor, why make such a dangerous effort? But this accusation had fallen on deaf ears. Once more, Dr. Eicher found it a necessity to force these kinds of irritations out of his mind.

The face of the clock had now reached two in the afternoon. Why had she not yet arrived? He found himself on his main sofa engaging in nervous habits such as toe-tapping and compulsively moving about the room. Not until four did he hear a conveyance panel being opened.

Peering out of the blinds in the front room, Dr. Eicher's eyes bulged from their sockets; she appeared just as he had been imagining it in those four long hours, elegantly dressed in robes of satin and silk. She was helped from her locomotive hand in hand by her dutiful servant, and she took a quick moment to glance around at the fairgrounds. A young man was accompanying her, and the doctor guessed that he was probably some relation.

The boy began to clamor at the interior of the carriage to climb out; however, the servant had seized him by the arm. This was to be a strictly private conversation with all matters of seriousness in contention.

Our glamorous lady, the Countess Ms. Joanne Freeman, was making her way up the drive. She was a woman of a relatively small yet curvaceous stature, which boasted a much larger presence in her gallant stride. Her azure irises stood out tremendously in the overcast setting, paired with long locks that resembled a blinding light of life. She wore a single piece of jewelry, a gold necklace, with her first name attached—hanging in a similar fashion.

Dr. Eicher waited eagerly for her to call upon him, and he waited at the door with his hand firmly on its handle. Three polite, quick rings of the house bell and he opened to meet her face-to-face.

"Doctor! Thank you so much for meeting me on such short notice."

She had waited for him to show her through the entrance, and he did so with an unusually low bow.

"The pleasure is all mine, of course. Please let us sit down in the tearoom." Dr. Eicher's body shook with rapture.

The pair walked together through the foyer and into the main sitting area, fully furnished and awaiting its master's return. Ms. Freeman had previously been a patient of the doctor's; however, she had not been to see him in quite some time. They had been friendly and cordial, for Dr. Eicher gave her what she would claim to be inspiring advice, and they had written small notes to each other a few times before the countess had left on important orders regarding her father's estate. As his nervous habits implied, the doctor was simply smitten by her presence.

There had been a long pause before the doctor—attempting to run with a clear, open opportunity for conversation—inquired, "Ms. Freeman, is this a matter of your dear father? Is he well?"

Joanne Freeman's head drooped. "Oh yes . . . yes, he is quite well. I had almost nothing to do with the meeting at all. I know not why they had summoned me for such a blasé diction."

"That is most wonderful to hear."

Ms. Freeman was less than enthused, so the doctor led her into more personal issues.

"What, if I may not so subtly inquire, is the purpose of this visit then?" He thought it wise to be honest and less formal with her so that she might reveal her true intention.

"I have been thinking, most grievingly, about the direction to which my life has been leading."

Silence passed for a moment or two.

"Dear Countess, I am a man learned in the psychological arts. Do not hesitate to bring what you wish to light. I may be able to help you understand."

She spoke no words again. He was at a loss for speech himself and had not a moment to mull over her vagueness when she simply started to sob.

"Erich, my trusted Erich. I have been haunted by the evil questions of the nonphysical world. I know not why I am so alone. I feel that even close companions and family dread my company. I forever wonder what it is like to have someone stationed at my side who will not stray away at my uncontrollable needs and wants."

Capitalizing on this genuine expression, Dr. Eicher insisted, "But I . . . I am here for you, Ms. Freeman! As I will repeat, you can divulge to me anything you wish." This was not an empty promise by any means, but secretly, his ulterior motives shunted him from the concrete facts. He had been focusing on her appearance more than he could focus on his own practices.

"You are most unfailing in your kindness, Erich. Perhaps we could continue this at length another day? I must be going now, for young Peter has his language and mathematics lessons, and I must accompany him."

A bit agitated at the stalling of his progress, Dr. Eicher nonetheless broke into speech, "But of course, Ms. Freeman. Whenever you wish to continue, I will clear my day's activities."

"Wonderful! Simply wonderful. I shall call to you within a fortnight." Joanne's face brightened considerably, and she curtsied as they approached the entrance hallway.

Then, without the doctor noticing it for a short interval, she had held up her hand to him in earnest for him to take it and place a peck on top of it. He did so with composure, not too long or too aggressively as to show her his confidence and sincerity. With this goodbye, she only smiled and made her way back to her servant driver, and she was off.

His chest began to burn the instant the carriage drew around the first corner of the cobblestone. It was as though hot coal that had burned for hours on the fireplace was shoved firmly against his sternum. However romantic this appeared to be, compared with the brevity of the topics spoken, Dr. Eicher was not so familiar with this feeling. It had been nothing but a lust for the hand of a captivating individual. He wanted very much to pick up a quill and piece of parchment to write his deepest desires about her, but to tell her his full list of emotions would certainly be out of line. Instead, he thought it best to do nothing.

Aside from pondering the possibility of him breaking his unspoken patient-doctor confidentiality, the course of his passion had bled out to resemble a muse for his upcoming venture.

I will write about the stunning Joanne!

This was to the doctor an ideal brainstorm, for he could push his obsession without ever properly acting on it. After the competition was over, he could reveal to her his layout of fact and infatuation to convince her to accept his advances.

Fumbling over to his unofficial workspace in the corner of the now dimly lit, sunset-pierced room, he began to stare deep into a blank and blinding sheet of paper in front of him. He had not even begun to press the ink upon its writing surface when he began to marshal his thoughts on the makeup of that which had just left footprints in the very space around him. He believed Joanne was with him in the room. He bore the resemblance of a sick man unable to notice his surroundings after being in hospital for an injury that required heavy medication. His neurotic connections were outweighing the physical form that was no longer present. He began to picture a large field of agricultural starches spanning miles in east and west direction. However, deciding to stroll due north, the landscape became continually barren. Hard frost overtook the warm summer he had not a minute ago just been experiencing.

To his surprise, in an immediate change of scenery, a great glacier in an icy ocean had popped up in front of his person. This sight, captivating as it was, was slowly showing signs of deterioration. He could see it melting ever so rapidly, and the marshy dirt at his feet was becoming sodden in flood. He peered down into the body of water before him and noticed that, as it was clearly himself staring back, his reflection did not fully resemble himself. Determined to feel the warmth of the great plains behind him, he turned heel to utter shock. The field was torched with flame. Now, caught between two odd portrayals of dilapidation, he sat in a state of bewilderment at the fact that he was now trapped in a state of euphoric purgatory.

The doctor raised his cranium with less than a startle from the glow reappearing through the half-drawn curtains in the sitting room. Beads of sweat were stationary upon only his forehead and on his breast, indicated by the deep gray of his undershirt. Thinking that these dreams were certainly becoming a greater burden than usual, he began to steady himself, as to remove himself from his seat, and began the mechanical process of preparing for his watch with Mr. Esche.

As a man who could deduce complexities in mental processing, Dr. Eicher understood that this dream, and a poor laconic effort, had been at the mercy of his thoughts about Joanne. As revelation began to take shape of semiexistent plausibility, mingled with derision of his own situational ostentatiousness, the bulb of truth seemed to flicker easily in his frontal lobe. What else could it have possibly been? A quiet ailment that crept up into one's livelihood. He had been distracted all this time and for good measure. He was hard-pressed to find another reason for it because he truly wished and believed it was so. He might not have had many words to present about her, but his nerves could not have produced anything remotely physical to that seismic comparison of her physical being.

Pleased with this conclusion, the doctor watched his driver arrive around the same corner of the block Joanne

Freeman had traced half a day ago and felt that his profound yearning would grasp his objective of winning the heart of Joanne and the mind of Arnold Esche simultaneously.

At this point in time, our dedicated journeyman by the name of Archibald Cunnings had arrived at the Downington train station with an air of nervous contempt. He had been wondering all night, while laying his head to rest, if he was going on nothing but an excursion to test his loyalties. Although he wanted very much to attain *The Absolute Watch* and be its chief operator, he could not shake the fact that it seemed too great of a trip and much too much trouble for a man of his education to embark on a faux wild goose chase for an inanimate object.

Removing a chocolate-colored leather coffer from his personal carriage, he shuffled up to the platform of the rustic boxcar tracks. As the steam engine made its way around the first bend out of the station, he had, once and for all, decided that his goal was paramount and that no more questions would arise in his mind to steer him away from doing what needed to be done.

Just before boarding the train, having to hop onto the incline of stairs to reach the entrance to the car, he glanced over to a haggard-looking man in a black cloak struggling to do the same. As he watched, a conductor pulled the man up by his collar into the said compartment, designated for engineers. Thinking this was a happenchance occurrence, he continued into the hallway of the car and checked his ticket that Arnold had purchased for him to make sure he had correctly chosen his place among the others scattered in and between the rows of first-class seats in front of him.

During the frigid yet bright morning, Dr. Eicher had arrived earlier than usual to work—because of his lack of sleep and eagerness—to begin his writing and to present a synopsis of his ideas to Arnold. His coworker Pierre Libois slipped into the conference room without the doctor noticing. The doctor was occupied by surreptitiously penning his initial thoughts. As soon as he noticed Pierre out of the corner of his eye, he raised his head to meet him face-to-face.

With a burst of confidence, Mr. Libois exclaimed, "How exciting it is to be engaged in our first brainstorm together!"

The two men had met on professional occasions before; however, much less was at stake, and Arnold had dictated almost all the rhetoric. Dr. Eicher gave a swift nod and continued to scribble notes.

Noticing the doctor was busy with his own tendencies, he began to talk out into the room as if he was listening attentively.

"I wonder if Arnold will give us any suggestions on how we should format our ideas. Or perhaps he will ask us to give him information on it himself? That would be splendid! I really can't imagine what kind of advice we can exchange."

All the while Pierre was speaking, the doctor had been paying attention, but only just enough so that he might catch the hint that the former would cease. Pierre was being much too open with his language, and he would certainly not attain a place among Arnold Esche's favorability if he kept up the charade. The doctor mentally noted that this irksomeness was a part of Pierre's character but that to shoot him down at such a high point of stimulation would only increase the chance of an unwanted friction.

Peering down at the inkblots and feeling mildly satisfied, for this was the penmanship of a critical man, Erich laid his hand to rest to take a firm look at Mr. Libois.

Having his full attention now, Mr. Libois asked, "Would you be interested in that kind of interaction?"

Not having grasped the question but wanting to remain polite and thoughtful, Erich agreed.

"Wonderful! I do hope you'll accept this brochure I have concocted." Reaching across the table, Pierre handed Dr. Eicher a pamphlet.

A quick, nonchalant acceptance found this booklet in Erich's pocket, with no interest in reading it immediately.

Taking no notice of this action, Pierre began speaking on its creation for another minute or two until, at nine o'clock, Arnold Esche whisked the doors of the meeting room wide open and marched to the head of the table. The two men currently seated around the table now gave their full attention to their surroundings, and both realized that Archibald was not present.

As Arnold began his premeditated speech, Pierre eagerly inquired, "But, Mr. Esche, where is dear Archibald?"

Dr. Eicher started to gather wind to answer.

However, Arnold, having broken across the stillness of the air, blurted, "Mr. Cunnings will be traveling out of the country for quite some time. This is, of course, due to this little experiment of ours!"

A chain of connections began processing in the mind of the doctor.

"He will have no point of contact because he will be far away in the East, but do not worry! He is a man of great talent, and I have one-hundred-percent confidence that he will return safely."

As there was great emphasis on the last word of his sentence, Erich took the last word as a foreboding.

"But, Mr. Esche, how can we discuss discourse with one of our most important members absent?"

"We will have to manage with the three of us of course! We are all highly capable individuals. Now, since

I have called this get-together, I shall discuss my plans for this business while you two are well occupied."

Dr. Eicher and Pierre Libois leaned forward in their seats in earnest, for this would determine the direction in which they would possibly follow suit.

"As you know, I have spoken about writing for *The Absolute Watch* myself, an idea that you have all had been wary of. So after much deliberation and consideration, I have decided that I will remain a simple overseer of its information and progression."

The doctor breathed a sigh of relief. Erich, looking toward Pierre for his reaction, saw that he remained quite still.

"Now that I have shared what little I have been thinking about in regard to profession, I would love to hear what you both can bring to the table, both physically and in terms of progressive ideas of course!"

Before discussion arose on who was to present their findings first, Pierre rose from his place and began making his way to the head of the table, much like Arnold Esche had done a few minutes previously upon his entrance. Pierre cleared his throat, steadied himself, and then began his annunciation.

"Gentlemen, man himself has been thrown into this world as a foremost player in his environment. Humans alike have dreamed and planned events to continue this natural selection. As an individual, he holds a certain power of influence over his own actions and thoughts. The individual is a model that we can plainly see before ourselves because he is present before us. What we cannot see are his motivations. We cannot see his thought processes and the way he wishes to carry out his desperate desires.

"This, gentlemen, is the greatest problem that we may face in what is called the tangible plane. The subjective plane, however, hides its truths in the deepest part of one's neurons. It is not something that can be grabbed. It must be lured out of its hiding place. What do we as individuals use as a lure to hook these tendencies and premeditations to bring them to light? I dare say, it is easy to come up with a solution! Other individuals. We, again as humans, are alike in many a way. Our most primal ideals are the barest of them all when it comes to necessities. The gateway to the *Homo sapiens'* way of life is built through intermingled interaction between individuals. When we find such common ground, only then are we truly at peace with ourselves as well as our ways. If this were a false claim, the term would be *Homo sapien*—the singular form of the word that does not exist.

"I am sorry if it seems that I am off topic, however I do have a final thought to which Mr. Esche has kindly brought us here today. My proposal for this project of ours is to put together a group of individuals. Individuals who share not only basic similarities and differences but who are socially connected as well. *The Absolute Watch* has provided myself with great insight into this matter, and I would like to explore it in greater detail if it is approved. Thank you for your time, gentlemen."

Arnold Esche stood up immediately from his place in Mr. Libois's previously vacant seat and began to clap voraciously.

"My dear Mr. Libois! That is a splendid topic to present to me. Do you have any physical aspects to add to this theory of yours?"

"Indeed, I do." Pierre handed Mr. Esche the same pamphlet he had given to Dr. Eicher while the latter was preparing his notes. The title read, "Common Practice."

After being relieved of his false excitement, Mr. Esche had gestured for the doctor to present his initial thoughts on the subject at hand. Walking slowly up to the place where Mr. Libois had been standing moments before, Dr. Eicher spoke from what little he had written about that so enveloped his attention.

"Mr. Esche, in a man's life, he comes before many things that become a distraction to him. If he is conscious of the matter, he does his best to move forward and complete the tasks he wishes to at hand. If he becomes engulfed in the distraction, then he will lose his objective goals and give in to a certain sickness. He does not loathe this unwellness, but it becomes all he knows. It becomes the only thing he thinks about. It becomes the only thing he dreams about. The only solution is to avoid this malady. Avoid it at all costs. If he can do this, then he has what remaining time he has been allowed by himself to pursue other interests. These other interests are distractions as well, but they are much less harmful and time-consuming than the obsessive sickness.

"When this infirmity presents itself in human form, it has a greater pull than any other that the individual has within himself. I am not entirely certain of this ultimatum, but I have been led to believe it is so. Not only through personal experience, but through observation of others as well. I ask you if I may write about a certain individual. This person I have studied well, and I believe I can deduce social norms and aspirations through the said person. In this way I hope to become the operator of this fine business. Thank you."

Again, Arnold arose in a flare of scorching applause. "Again, I have been presented with a fine focal point! Doctor, you will truly be a match for Mr. Libois."

At this supposition, Dr. Eicher and Pierre met each other's eyes, and both acknowledged a certain tense, impending excitement.

Mr. Esche gave some final thoughts on the matter. "The two of you, no doubt, have put not only time but effort towards your research. Dr. Eicher, I had almost forgotten, do you have anything physical to present about this muse of yours?"

Hesitant as he already was about Joanne, he merely slipped out, "I'd rather it be a secret, if you please."

Satisfied with the doctor's reply, Arnold continued, "I will give each of you, including Mr. Cunnings, two weeks to complete your work. This will bring us near the current year's end."

This was agreed upon by all parties present.

As the conversation dried up, Genevieve Allman walked past the threshold with Arnold's agenda for the workday. Dr. Eicher, feeling a bit lackluster, turned and headed out of the room. After Ms. Allman had finished briefing Arnold, he too took his leave. With Pierre Libois and Genevieve Allman left to themselves in the conference space, Mr. Libois attempted his first true acquisition.

"Ms. Allman, I do hope you and Mr. Esche have been able to settle your differences." He continued, flowing his sympathies. "Now that we are to engage in an attempt to take the reins of this place, I realize you may not feel as if fairness is truly playing its role here."

More irritated than willing to agree, she muttered, "It matters not to you anyway."

"On the contrary! It matters to me very much. Please look at this, and read it in your spare time."

In Pierre's hand was the third brochure he had presented to the members of *The Absolute Watch* to read, though he knew only one would give it proper consideration. She took the leaflet reluctantly to appease Pierre. Curious but still very calculating, Genevieve jumped from the paper to his eyes and quickly turned toward the exit.

Now alone in his chambers at the end of the day, Mr. Arnold Esche mulled over his prospective agenda for the next one. Moving aside various pieces of paperwork, Pierre Libois's "Common Practice" had fallen to the floor. Thinking it was of important value, he picked it up and turned it thrice in his hand. Thoughts sparked about earlier events that had occurred. As a cynical character, Mr. Esche believed that both men had been talking about him when they were discussing their respective projects. He knew he was a great influencer both of individuals and groups alike. Perhaps it was his business they were after? But of course. Either way, he gave the matter no more thought and did not bother to read Pierre's literature, as he had already chosen a successor, and that, in his strongest convictions, was all that truly mattered.

I break now from the novel to speak on its ever-forming direction. I pray that you, as investigative readers, have been paying close attention to the players in our story.

Arnold Esche, Archibald Cunnings, Pierre Libois, and Erich Eicher have been developing ever so slightly into the characters I've made them out to be. At this I am comforted, because I have been thinking on them for quite some time. As men, they possess a familiar air of masculinity and brute eagerness in their pursuits. Therefore, they have been so far prevalent and of utmost importance. However, another special person, Genevieve Allman, will transform into a character of greater prominence as we unfold the tale of *The Absolute Watch*. The similarities and differences of characters in their human habitat will take a greater physical form as well. This I hope you will consider, and in doing so, perhaps you will see the far-reaching extent of my ideas.

Many more characters will follow and fill in the socialization as in the tangible world. They are paramount, for the fact that they change and affect our major players. As well as similarities and differences, objective and subjective planes of existence will also be thinned or stretched out, warped, and constantly crossed. Here, there is a certain amount of mental ambiguity needed, and I hope that it is not all that confusing, although I know my train of thoughts may derail you at some point. Please, continue.

4

As nightfall began to dim the light over the face of the now-resting Archibald Cunnings, pure darkness soon followed, and the other riders present on the train began to bustle about the aisle in attempts to quiet the hunger pangs they felt in the pits of their stomachs. Slowly opening his eyes slightly to get a glimpse of his lashes and the soft artificial light inside the train, Archibald noticed that night had fallen and he, too, awoke with the same sensation in his abdomen. The minuscule amount of sleep had given him some time to relax and get used to the fact that he would be familiarized with this form of traveling in due time.

Peering out of the window next to his cushioned seat, he noticed the party had reached the countryside and that he was now in full pursuit of what he had promised to attain for Mr. Esche. Addressing his need for sustenance, he became comforted by the fact that the first-class dining car would have a lavish meal for himself to partake in.

Stretching out his limbs, he now began to steady himself upright and look about the crowd behind him. He noticed instantaneously that they were of some wealth, because of the way they were handsomely dressed. Brightly colored dresses and sharp suits were on prominent display. He took aim at a woman with a large pearl necklace who wore a hat seemingly ten times bigger than her head at first glance. Again he scanned about and found an old gentleman in a gray cloak sporting a large wooden cane donned with a type of well-cut jewel at its head. Focusing his vision, he realized that all of them were more than dressed appropriately and that they had shown great effort in their appearance.

Politely moving about the narrow corridor, he greeted them in passing with a cordial "Please" and "Not at all" until he found his way to the glass door that read, "Dining," in white, frosted lettering.

Sliding it open gingerly, he noticed that he was the first prospective diner to arrive at that minute. He closed the door behind him and began to make his way toward the many booths aligned on the left and right of the car. After walking past the barman and greeting him in a similar fashion as he had with the rest of the population still hovering around their seats, he spotted that curious gentleman once again. The man in the black cloak, now looking positively deranged and worrisome, seemed to be whispering to an apparition as he leaned over one of the tables. No one else seemed to notice him, and Archibald, not feeling the need to spoil his conversation, sat in near the front entrance, at the bar, well away from him.

Thumbing through the selection of provisions, he could not help but hear the man's conversation grow louder. Ignoring this fact, aware he should keep to himself, he continued flipping through the menu. However, curiosity had caught Mr. Cunnings by the scruff of the neck. First, he listened to decipher if the man was speaking in his native tongue. He was not. Second, he wondered if he could make out exactly what language the man was speaking in. Not so much to his surprise, it was Russian. Thinking to himself that the destination alone brought about this fact, he was satisfied and paid no more mind to him.

After receiving his nod from the barman, indicating he wasn't particularly in the mood for a drink, he unwillingly made his way to a secluded booth in the back of the car to attempt to choose a dish of his liking. As he passed the man in the black cloak, he noticed the man was grasping a full glass of clear liquid that ultimately had to be vodka. But of course, this was the reason the man was engaging in such behavior!

How was it that he was able to purchase a ticket? This was the question that now kept Archibald occupied as he took his seat and waited patiently for a service member to attend to him. *He must be of some rank to be able to afford this.*

Why has the barman clearly supplied this man's drink, knowing he was a bit out of control?

He pondered for a few moments before it had all come so rapidly into play. At that very moment, two men in conductors' uniforms threw open the door to the dining car and immediately strode over to the man in the black cloak. They each grabbed one of his arms and pried him out of the booth. Archibald hesitated momentarily as the black-cloaked man struggled to stay put.

Archibald then asked abruptly, attempting to defend him, "Excuse me, gentlemen, to what does this man owe the pleasure of your insolence?"

They both shot a look to Archibald's peeping head, and one of them scoffed, "Insolence? Ha! This idiot is our coworker! It's quite a shame he cannot be fired, but the least we can do is make sure he's sober when he begins his duties."

With that comment, the men dragged him away and into the first-class car. As they made their way down the aisle, head after head turned in dismay as they reached its end. He was then pushed into the front car for conductors, and as that door was pulled shut, the two men also disappeared behind it. Archibald watched all this from his seat, and only when the dining car door slid shut was his view of all the disruption finally obstructed.

In her father's vacant dwelling, Genevieve Allman was sitting in the small section of a dining room with one candle lit beside her. She had been lingering on the fact that this place of her childhood was now solely in her possession. Not a happy memory had passed through her mind on any occasion since her father's passing, although she knew that they might have existed. Andrew Allman had been a somewhat caring man though he could never quite put together an objective facet of that nature. He had told Genevieve on countless occasions that he cared for her more than life itself, a fate that any father should undertake in the raising and rearing of a daughter.

What more had he been willing to do to prove this? Nothing, she concluded.

However, the fact that his considerations had been spoken into existence had been enough for her to justify that it was ultimately true. She stood and made her way about the room, and her feet wandered in a circular motion. A few boxes of wood lay in the corner next to a worn, makeshift fireplace. These were the last remains and holdings of Andrew Allman. Genevieve had not yet brought herself to lay hands on these notes and records as of late because she did not care at all for her father's business endeavors—not because they had failed, but because she saw numbers and calculations as fallacies of disdain.

In a momentary spirit of inquiry, she shuffled over to them and stared down the hundreds of pages of documentation. Not a thing had been organized. She saw glimpses of production projections in the same place where employee time cards had been ever so sloppily punched.

"It all makes so much sense," she had coughed up out of the silence.

Late into the evening, she found herself dividing and conquering all the sheets that lay before her. She attempted to match categories unbeknownst to her to ones that she had been familiarized with. Accounting, human resources, and packaging and production were among the greatest topics that she had mustered and further separated from the small hand-notes and scribbles she had uncovered through the cluttered mess. After picking through the majority of the rough, she had noticed a sealed envelope at the bottom of one of the crates. It was worn, yet not torn, and looked like it had been passed through a pair of hands repeatedly. As she reached for it, turned it, and read in her mind the words "If Ever We'll Be" that were scrawled on its front, she opened it, peeling away the adhesive and unfolding the wrinkled paper.

She read aloud:

Dear Florence,

In my attempts to receive your attention, I have undoubtedly failed. Each time I gather what little strength I must have to approach you and speak my mind, I seem to falter and withdraw my courage. This is, without question, because you surpass me in all walks of life. You, whom I have come to see, not as a muse, but as a role model, prove that I, as a man, have no place whatsoever beside you. It is that simplicity that you so graciously radiate, that drives me to constantly melt away. It activates as soon as my eyes lay claim to your figure. At this, I am deeply saddened because it proves that I am not worthy to be with you. At this realization, I am unequivocally distraught. The only positive outcome I could foresee between us is that this icy feeling that arises may numb this wound that I am all too aware is present. I am forever in your debt, although I owe you nothing, and the same is true as is with reciprocation. If this limited view is somehow evaded, I only pray that it blossoms into something that can grow year-round and cannot be harmed by weather or any other act of God. I apologize now for having even written this because of how childish it may sound, but if you could ever forgive me for having penned it, that would be enough of a comfort because at least then it would have met your boundless, universal vision.

Ever thine,

Andrew Allman

As Genevieve finished speaking the last words of her late father, the silence in the room grew even eerier and lonelier than before. She sat back down at her place next to the candle, which now only possessed a faint glow about it, for wick and flame had been surrounded by melting wax on all sides. She lit another to give the room a full look of basking light.

Thinking arduously about what she read, she left the letter on the table next to her copy of "Common Practice" that Pierre had given to her that afternoon. After another hour of filing and organizing the last bit of Andrew's belongings, she sat back down once more and flipped her vision from her father's letter to Pierre's pamphlet. As she was picking both up to store them away, the latter had fallen open. It was blank. Wondering if it was merely her pupils playing tricks on her in the lateness of the hour, she set her full attention to the pamphlet.

On the front, "Common Practice" was clearly labeled, and this she already knew. Putting down her father's letter, with both hands free, she opened the pamphlet and saw that on the inside panels, not a thing was written. Confused, though not entirely convinced, she put it adjacent to the burning candle for better reading light. Blank.

Why did he purposely leave the whole thing blank? she wondered.

Genevieve sat back down and compared the two pieces of writing, this time carefully examining and scanning them as though they would leave her sight. Over and over, she thought of what they had done differently in penmanship, although the two couldn't have been any more different. She began reasoning critically because she could not get over the fact that although they were both different, they had some minor similarities. Then, as it pushed into the frontal lobe of her brain, she finally extrapolated the very thing she had been debating for that short period of dense processing. She quickly leaped up from her place to grab one of the ink pens that she had found beside her father's paperwork and opened Pierre's offering. On the left-hand side, she wrote "Similarities." On the right-hand side, "Differences."

Next morning, in the dark before daybreak, Pierre Libois turned the lock on the front door of *The Absolute Watch* and crept in so slothfully that you would have believed he would be waking others from slumber. The front lobby was even blacker than the dim light outside, so he had paused for a moment staring ahead to adjust his pupils to appropriate his vision. As he heaved and drew breath, for the bitter cold of winter was now upon Downington, he contemplated the slew of events that were to come.

First, of Arnold and his professional career that was ever so dear to him. Second, of the doctor, for he knew that this man was his greatest rival to date. Third, of Genevieve, because he knew she was his ticket to achieve every theory he had never been able to properly prove to himself. These three points of interest swirled about menacingly in his head. For what seemed like a particularly long time, he ran over them in earnest. His blood flow increased with every high, and every low seemed to force the extremities on his hands to clench into fists.

Eventually, with much effort, he was able to clear his mind, deeply exhale, and move about the rest of the establishment. He strode along the corridors and brushed his hand against the white walls as he turned their perpendicular lengths. Being as empty as this place was, for he was clearly the first to arrive for the day's work, it felt as bleak a void as ever. He truly was a ghost that was haunting the halls. Quite present, although to no witnesses, he could proceed to accomplish whatever he wished by his own means, producing no qualms that could stop his mind's eye.

He was heading toward the area of *The Absolute Watch* where the freelance writers and editors sat penciling away at columns that they wished completed. Here was where all the information was gathered to dictate a paper that reached the vision of many a man and woman. Pieces that covered various topics such as advice, food, fashion, sport, humor, and critical review. A color wheel of human interaction lay beautifully before any reader who wished to purchase a copy and comb it. Pierre, who was very much conscious at this, felt proud that such substance could arise from a standpoint to which he was thoroughly involved. His employer affected countless individuals' day-by-day activities to such a degree that to not be honored by this truth would certainly enact a stain of ignorance upon him. He certainly would not stand to let that happen! This was exactly the conclusion to which he had arrived. After all, if he were to head this newspaper, he must show Arnold, as well as the rest of his employees and colleagues, that this ideal of community in *Homo sapiens* could never exist in the form of the singular sense.

Mr. Libois entered the open space of chairs and writers' desks and glanced around, noticing various materials scattered about them. He spotted a large corkboard that hung adjacent to the door of the editor-in-chief, which was emblazoned with stenciled paper letters that spelled out T-O-P H-E-A-D-L-I-N-E-S. He studied the room for another moment or so, having stumbled for a second over his own feet, and eventually made his way to the board. Only a few small scraps of paper were stuck in the tacks to which they had been secured. Pierre reached into his coat pocket and retrieved the brochure he had already given to Arnold, Erich, and Genevieve. A second piece of paper followed. This was a note that had been handwritten by Mr. Libois, and it read as follows:

> To: Members of *The Absolute Watch*,
> Every employee wishing to hone their skills in human understanding, please report to the main conference room at 7PM sharp this evening. Thank you.

Removing some of the tacks with the tiny, ripped pieces of paper on them and tossing them into a waste bin, Pierre fastened both the brochure and the letter side by side to the cork and thought to himself as he completed this, *Surely, I will have a few interested minds that will inquire.*

He turned on the spot and made his way through the room to the entrance that now became his exit. Pierre repeated this task throughout the rest of the workplace in accounting, human resources, and packaging and production. After its completion, the sun had just begun to rise over the lowest section of windows of *The Absolute Watch*. Indeed, it was a cold, bitter morning. However, there was an air of opportunity that seemed to grace Pierre Libois as he headed toward the top floor of the building to his office. With much paperwork waiting in the wings, he was most confident that his real work had just begun.

As she arrived for work in the basking light, Genevieve Allman drew the opening of her coat closer together as a breeze of blustery air slipped around her. She was running late, which was nothing unusual, as her profession was not strictly time-expedient. There was nothing particularly different about this morning, but when she awoke, she had felt that somehow, something had been awry. As she had opened the front doors to *The Absolute Watch*, she had noticed that one of Arnold's staff clerks had not been there to hand her the schedule of the day.

Quite odd, she pondered.

Nonetheless, she had made her way through the very same halls and corridors Pierre had followed earlier that morning right up to the editing room, where he had first pinned his brochure and letter to *The Absolute Watch* employees. She poked her head into the room to see almost every one of them huddled together like herrings in a barrel.

"An important meeting, I suppose," she whispered to herself.

Paying no more attention to the event, she headed for Arnold's study where he would surely still be sleeping if no staff clerk was moving about the building with reels of information to busy him with. She approached the large oak door to find a brown envelope attached to its handle dangling from a piece of brown string. Her name was in neat cursive on the front. She made a move for the peephole near the top of the door to an obvious inversion that narrowed her sight.

Without further curiosity, she removed the envelope from the handle and slid out the paperwork inside; it was the schedule for the day's work. She began shuffling the script page by page until she had noticed a slightly thinner piece that stuck out on the upper-left-hand side. It was a note written by hand.

Before reading it, she said aloud, "Obviously, this will explain the constant absences I have come across so early."

Putting the rest of the pages of the schedule into the envelope and placing them under her arm, she began to walk toward the main conference room and narrated the lines in her mind:

> Dear Genevieve,
>
> As you may have already noticed, I am absent. This is due to my own personal device, and it will be some time before I return. I am to be meeting with foreign diplomats by order of the Board of Governors of The Commerce and Wealth of England to foster lucrative relationships with businesses abroad. This

task I am taking on is to be my greatest achievement yet! I only hope that you understand and wish me well in my endeavor. I have presented you with today's schedule in hopes that you will model it for daily forthcomings in the immediate future. Since you are my closest associate and can handle such volumes of work, I leave you in charge of all these operations until I return from my dealings. Do not fear, I have called upon Dr. Eicher to check in on the paper every so often as to oversee those things are run to my liking. Please oblige by the guidelines I have written. If you do so, everything will turn out to be copacetic.

Best regards,

Arnold Esche

So I am to bear the burden of all this labor? While others go about their regular and rehearsed motions? Most inequitable. This was the immediate reaction of Genevieve. *Dr. Eicher will oversee it all? As if that man does anything but think!*

Mulling over these new, potential repressions, she calmed herself and went in the direction of the conference room to get started on revamping the schedule given her.

Throughout the remainder of the business hours at *The Absolute Watch*, a buzz began to build. Conversations between staff members slowly shifted toward the mystery of who in their ranks was bold enough to house an idea that they were all almost certainly familiar with in regard to humanity.

In the accounting department, they drew witticism from the message they had received.

An accounts receivable clerk joked, "If humans truly understood their nature, they would be able to pay their bills!"

A financial manager strongly opposed such topics being discussed. "Numbers are the true key to understanding this existence. It is what makes up our objective universe! Someone means to tell us that we as the people are made of natural progressions."

Skepticism followed in even greater numbers in the area of human resources. A personal assistant to one of the officers had made mention to her that a certain someone believed they had the key to a greater understanding of personal matters.

She merely scoffed, "All there is to know is what we observe daily. No underlying factors could possibly apply. We come and do our business, say our piece, and go about our lives as simply as the twenty-four hours we are given ticks along."

The assistant reluctantly agreed with her; perhaps this was because he didn't want to steer away from his duties and cause friction for someone in such a delicate position. In packaging and production, not much thought was given on the matter. When the men and women of this department saw the writing Pierre had anonymously placed upon their announcement board, they believed it to be one of the other departments' doing and rightfully dismissed it, due to it not concerning those who had no business in interdepartmental communication. When their manager saw it tacked upon their corkboard—the man who worked directly under Pierre—he took it down, glanced upon it, and promptly threw it away, for he was keen on having a clean and clear area.

Many more discussions ensued as the afternoon moved into the early hours of the evening. Most of the individuals of *The Absolute Watch* concluded, for reasons unbeknownst to us, that to be involved in a learning process after a laborious workday would be too great a mission.

As they began to file out of the front doors, Pierre Libois sat waiting in the conference room. He had been here most of the day, after he had seen Genevieve Allman vacate the premises earlier that morning. As the clock moved ever so slowly to seven, he became more and more anxious.

What if no one was to attend? Surely, someone must. The predictability is in favor of the odds.

Pierre knew that if even one person were to arrive, eager to hear what he had to say, he could certainly run this business. Then, as the wooden door to the conference room creaked open, a young man's head appeared in the same manner as one sought to make an appearance where he was not wanted. Pierre made eye contact with him. It was one of Arnold Esche's staff clerks. He pushed his way through the entrance and stood in repose, apparently waiting to be spoken to. Pierre, noticing this and much aware this was how Arnold handled his personal affairs, let the first words out.

"Yes, dear boy, what have you to say?"

The young man walked over to him and held out a piece of parchment. He began, "This, Mr. Libois, is a note from Mr. Esche. It was made to make its way to Dr. Eicher, but I am afraid I was curious and took the liberty of opening it and reading it, although I should not have." Disappointment was prominent in the last five words spoken.

Receiving the letter with delicacy, as to not snatch it away from him, Pierre opened it and moved about the lines from left to right with his pertinent vision.

> Dr. Eicher,
>
> I hope that you are well. This letter has been written on the account of current events that have changed in my favor. One that will affect you in the same manner, I am sure. I have been called upon by the Board of Governors of The Commerce and Wealth of England to travel abroad and meet with foreign dignitaries to foster business relations. In my place, I am asking you to head *The Absolute*

Watch for the time being. You do not need to worry yourself with the physical running of the paper because I have left those duties to Genevieve. All I ask for you to do is oversee everything that goes on here. By this, I mean for you to carefully inspect all activity that goes on in my absence and report it to me. I will be the first to make contact so that my location is not a mystery to you. I ask you to respond promptly so the reply will not be lost between my movements. I understand that you may have other things on your mind now, but please do not undertake this task in vain. It is imperative that I have knowledge of what is happening at *The Absolute Watch*.

Best regards,

Arnold Esche

PS. Please do keep a close eye on Genevieve. I trust in her, but at times she has been known to go about things in her own manner. I do not want her getting the idea that she has control over the direction and dictation of the other employees. Second, if for any reason there is an emergency, please do not hesitate to take whatever action you see fit to control it. My faith in you is steadfast.

After finishing the calligraphy penned by Arnold, Pierre investigated the face of the youth and asked him his name.

Clearing his throat and poising himself upright, he said, "Sebastian, sir." He seemed proud to be asked this question. Someone as lowly as a staff clerk was speaking directly with one of the business's figureheads after all.

"Very good, very good." Pierre was now formulating the true purpose of his inquiry. "Sebastian, is there a chance that you have already shown this letter to either Genevieve or Dr. Eicher?"

Sebastian thought about his answer for a moment or two, attempting to decipher if the honest answer was truly the best answer. After deciding that it most certainly was, he replied, "No, I have not. Ms. Genevieve had been tardy this morning, and it had slipped my mind to bring it to her attention because it was not for her after all. Dr. Eicher, on the other hand, was not here today, so there was no chance of me leaving it around for someone else's eyes to find. You being the next ranking official, I concluded that it should be brought to you when I had completed my other duties."

These were Pierre's sentiments as well, and he was thrilled that the boy had taken such responsibility seriously. Could it be that he could be trusted although this was their first personal encounter?

Nodding his head approvingly, Pierre continued, "Very well. Sebastian, would it be too much for me to ask something of you? A favor regarding official business?"

Immediately, after hearing the word *official* proceeded by *business*, Sebastian reacted with enthusiasm, "Indeed you can, sir! What exactly is the next course of action?"

Seemingly putting all his eggs into one small basket, Pierre began his speech. "If you do not find it against your own personal code of ethics, would you mind not delivering this to Dr. Eicher or mention it to Genevieve? I am conducting an experiment that requires great uninterrupted research."

Before he could continue, Sebastian belted out, "You mean the workshop you are attempting to put together about human understanding?"

Pausing to register the youth's comment, he broke out in eagerness, "Exactly the point! I am glad someone had noticed my intentions. Yes, I feel as though this piece of writing would be conflicting in my personal attempts."

As Pierre glanced back at the note handed to him by the boy, Sebastian had been thinking about Arnold Esche and the way he had conducted his happenings while he was a staff clerk these many months. Arnold had lost temper with him on several occasions and had threatened him more than a few times, though never actually engaging him in a physical manner or giving him the ax. Obviously not appreciative of these encounters, Sebastian decided it was time to seek other options.

"I can promise you that it will not be given to the doctor or spoken of publicly. I will do my best to ensure this."

Elated, yet keeping a collected air, Pierre motioned for him to sit at the conference table. They chatted about informal topics.

Pierre then reassured Sebastian, "By the way, I will be writing in Dr. Eicher's place so that all of this will run like clockwork. Please do your best to receive Arnold's letters and deliver them to my possession. If at any time someone, other than the doctor or Genevieve, should find it, it should be delivered to you, as it will be addressed to your attention."

"Of course, sir." Sebastian was satisfied that he now was finally being respected in the manner he thought deserved to someone who showed such due diligence.

5

That very same evening that Pierre Libois's plan had begun to formulate, Dr. Eicher sat alone at his residence, unsuccessfully deciding on how he should go about his own. Visions of Joanne Freeman had almost become a nuisance to him. The doctor spent most of the day pondering what little he knew about her. He could not seem to format thoughts into something worthy of his predilection. He focused on her appearance, the focal point of his research, but this did not seem to be enough to spawn a properly built proposal. Removing himself from a writing desk with great force, as he had done constantly the whole afternoon through, he began pacing about the room.

Befuddled as he was already, he began to engage in scenarios of himself canoodling and wooing this woman with great metaphysical dwelling. Why did he care for this woman so much though he knew almost nothing about her? Why did she have such pull over his thoughts and actions to the point that they were bothersome?

If the doctor were performing an extraction of meaning from a patient, rather than himself, he would surely have been able to come to a reasonable and logical conclusion. But the very thought of this brought him nothing but further anguish. He only knew he wanted to be in her presence and assist her in any way he could.

Furthermore, Joanne Freeman was his topic in the matter of gaining Arnold's respect so that he could reach his objective. Dr. Erich Eicher had shirked his responsibilities at *The Absolute Watch* to begin chipping away to the core of his steadfast belief that the individual was the key to human understanding. If he could not prove this—and he believed Joanne the catalyst—then he surely would not succeed, and either Pierre Libois or Archibald Cunnings would surely surpass him.

I need more time, his meditation echoed out in silence.

He began to pen a letter, explaining his thinking to Arnold so that the latter would afford him ample opportunity to sustain his work.

> Dear Arnold,
>
> I understand that a business must be run in a manner that brings together both expediency and efficiency, however if I am to complete the task that you have laid before the three of us, I am afraid I will need a great deal of opportunity to craft it outside of the workplace. I am asking you for an

undisclosed amount of time away from *The Absolute Watch*. I ask you in earnest because I am having a degree of difficulty getting outside of my own head to objectify my explanations. Please answer me promptly with your decision.

Your associate,

Dr. Erich Eicher

Satisfied with his plea for a greater degree of contingency, the doctor once again sat down at his desk to work tediously—writing, crossing out, then rewriting ideas that would ignite some sort of order in his operations. He sat with a single candle burning by his side until the melted wax had dripped a droplet or two onto his desk, alerting him that he needed another to take its place. As he motioned to a cabinet that included these sources of light, he heard a rapping on his front door. Taken aback, for it must have been a quarter or so to midnight, he quickly swapped out the old candle for the new, struck a match to flint, touched it to the wick, and set about for the door.

Taking a second to run his hand through his hair, he opened the door a smidgen, for it was freezing outside, and called, "To whom do I owe this late-night pleasure?"

"It is I, Edward Montclair."

The man paused, and not recognizing the name, the doctor flouted, "Sorry, I am not familiar with the said person, good night."

But just as he was about to close the small window of communication between them, the man beyond the obstruction spit out, "I come on behalf of Joanne Freeman!"

Stopping himself from pushing the wooden structure shut, Dr. Eicher pulled it past him and was now face-to-face with this man Edward Montclair—a prepossessing figure who was dressed in the finest cottons and sporting a monocle in one hand and a velvet top hat in the other. Perplexed, thinking he was a suitor or someone similar, the doctor stared reproachfully at him before Mr. Montclair spoke.

"I come bearing a letter from the honored and respected countess herself, Joanne Freeman. She had given me this letter not an hour ago to be delivered to one Dr. Erich Eicher. Would you happen to be that said gentleman?"

Now grasping the purpose of this stranger's visit and the unintimidating tone with which he addressed him, Dr. Eicher quickly motioned for him to pass through the threshold and into the foyer.

Turning on the spot, Dr. Eicher now welcomed him, "Yes, I am that person in particular! Thank you for traveling at this hour, especially in this chill, for it is most unpleasant!"

Mr. Montclair gave a shallow bow, replacing the monocle and hat to their proper areas of contact, and pulled out a letter from his front pocket and placed it in his opposing hand. He motioned a second time to his frock coat and pulled out another piece of paper from the inner linings. Clearing his throat, Edward Montclair read aloud.

> My dearest Erich,
>
> Please accept this invitation to a soiree at my father's estate this coming New Year. I would be honored if you would accompany me. Please note that this is a formal occasion, and all matters of dress should be respectful and professional. I am looking forward to your reply. In lieu of a physical acceptance, you may voice your decision to Mr. Montclair. I am looking forward to meeting with you soon.
>
> Forever grateful,
>
> Joanne Freeman

After finishing the last words of the invitation, Dr. Eicher replied, "Certainly, certainly, I will attend!"

Mr. Montclair nodded in acknowledgment. He then handed the doctor the second piece of parchment and turned on the spot to leave.

Dr. Eicher called out, "Thank you! Thank you!" as Mr. Montclair strolled down the pathway to his carriage.

When he was once again alone, the doctor darted to his desk, where the second candle now burned brightly. Carefully turning up the edges on the envelope, which read "Dr. Erich Eicher," on its front, he opened the trifold document and combed the letter ravenously.

It proclaimed:

My most trusted Erich,

I am sorry to have written this letter to you at all, for it reveals a side of me that I am not so familiar with myself. I write this late at night because this is when I am most troubled. Being left alone to question my own thoughts is starting to haunt me. I am anxious and sad simultaneously, and that has become a most unrecognizable feeling. I wish to act on my thoughts and feelings, but I am hindered by their completion. A constant high is followed by a constant low. My father is pressuring me into family affairs—my anxiety; but I am also aware that my relations are not all that fond of me— my sadness. I have a vision of equilibrium; however, I am not sure how to achieve it. I have tried many things to cope with this conundrum, but I know for certain I cannot attain it on my own. Please come to my residence as soon as you have the time, for I know you are a busy man. Do not forget about me. I beg you.

From a heart that beats most timidly,

Joanne Freeman

As day broke next morning, Pierre Libois arrived at *The Absolute Watch* earlier than even he had intended. His premature punctuality prompted him to observe its operations a bit more closely. Who were the first people to arrive, and what was their status? But of course, he knew the staff clerks would be bustling in a half hour's time. The endgame was to understand the habits of each department by reviewing their work patterns and communications. Was it possible that the interconnection between them all was as proper as he had thought it to be? Pierre understood that the hierarchical system that was in place had kept this business in good standing, but he was not so sure it was perfectly choreographed to include some type of lament laced in its character.

He sat motionless on a chair in the main entrance hall for some moments contemplating this. He figured it best to drop off his belongings in the conference room upstairs to stride through the corridors without the burden of carrying them. Once again, he had become a specter bobbing about the empty halls of *The Absolute Watch*. He passed by a few departments, slowing his pace only to match a passing thought. Opening the large wooden doors, he moved into the conference room and lit a few candles that sat on the table. There were papers neatly shuffled into piles.

Upon examining them, Pierre noticed the brown envelope labeled "Genevieve" at its head.

Obviously, this is her doing, he deduced.

This seemed peculiar to him, because he himself had been stationed here for a length of time the night before. She must have arrived after him and stayed late too, due to the thickness of the parchment. He now realized how worn the lit candles were that he had activated, and simultaneously he noticed a gathering of dilapidated waxy figures in a box in the corner of the room. She certainly was dedicated and organized in carrying out her tasks; perhaps therefore Arnold had chosen her for such a monumental undertaking. If this was to be her headquarters in the future, Pierre knew at some point their respective projects would indefinitely intertwine. He placed his things neatly on one of the chairs, the one situated at the head of the table, and made for the large oak doors back to the entrance hall.

As he returned to the front doors of the establishment, he noticed that the staff clerks had finally amassed in their usual, circular formation, gathering their news for the day so that they might fulfill all their duties. Pierre was halfway down the grand staircase when Sebastian and a few other young men and women noticed him. They all paid him a momentary glance then returned to their chattering.

Better their conversations remain unabridged, Pierre concluded to himself.

As *The Absolute Watch* began to fill up with its numerous constituents, Mr. Libois merely passed by with an open ear as to accustom himself to the mood that brewed upon officials and departments alike.

Down one hall he overheard a pair of accounting colleagues nonchalantly talking over budgeting.

"Why has no one submitted their plans for the end of this quarter? Do they not wish to continue their objectives for the new fiscal year?"

To which the next jeered, "Of course not. You know that every branch has no concept of money. They all think it grows upon foliage. Ironically, it is made of such material!"

The two jostled each other and continued about their way to their offices.

Pierre made note of the lack of seriousness for the rest of his brief stroll. Entering the eating quarters just below the offices, he overheard two groundskeepers arguing over who was to take on a particular piece of work.

"It is my time to rest! You should be the one to carry off the garbage and let me eat in peace!"

"After you have done nothing but roam the corridors and pick up scraps of paper? I was the one who was made to assist the visitors we had from the environmental sector. They gave me absolute hell and acted as if I was the main supervisor who had shown them my own poor and personal exertions."

"I apologize for the fact that you were commanded to complete a task not in your range of pay, but I'm afraid that is what has become of business today. Please leave me be. I only have but a quarter of an hour."

"Business to which I will no longer conduct with you!" The latter dropped a heap of old foodstuffs at the foot of the other and stormed off.

Having witnessed these occurrences, something Pierre had known was surely to happen in daily life, he was not so keen to accept them in the workplace. Professionalism should be conducted every second when one was among one's coworkers. If they were not, ultimately, at least chasing perfection, what was the point of showing up to work at all? These thoughts were bothering him when he heard troubled voices.

He turned a corner to where the human resources manager was located. The woman in charge was speaking to a production employee.

"I regretfully inform you that as of now, you have been terminated."

Pierre stopped short of the entrance and held his hand to his ear.

She continued, "We have numerical evidence that production has been down tremendously in this last quarter. As acting supervisor, you have incorrectly managed the field workers and have caused financial losses to this business."

Although he did not see who was standing on the inside of the door, Pierre knew to whom she was referring. It was his inferior, the man who worked directly under him.

"I understand that this situation is not ideal," the man began. "However, I am afraid that I have not been properly managed myself. Mr. Libois has been absent for some time in assisting me in my duties. I wonder if this is not at the root of the problem."

After a break in continued conversation over the matter, the woman announced, "Our main concern is that you did not act. You were fully aware of the troubles production was facing, and you did not do anything in your power to resolve them. This is enough reason for us to seek help elsewhere."

At these final words, Pierre slipped past the door and decided to make his way back to the conference room.

The entirety of this day was simply miserable for Genevieve Allman. Although things at *The Absolute Watch* were running smoothly, it came at a great cost to her physical well-being and peace of mind. She was constantly pacing the halls up and down, catering to leading officials as well as their immediate subordinates, attempting to assist them in any way she could.

In the human resources department, there was a query about who was to gather a list of names from all employees whose wages exceeded the median for the upcoming year. As this was most important for budgeting, an administrative assistant implored Genevieve to cater to it personally because he and his group were conducting that week's payroll. Reluctantly she agreed and was handed the necessary accommodations. What was considered the median was quite low.

She spent the first half of the day wrangling specific individuals, for some of them, much like her now, were constantly on the move. Other replies she had to send away for because a few people were on holiday and others had merely gone sick. Spending only a few moments at half day to break for sustenance, she was then called upon by the officer of the packaging department. When Genevieve arrived at her quarters, she looked most dreadful. This officer began to explain to Genevieve the news that one of her colleagues, the head of production, had been removed from his command. Genuinely shocked that this had been revealed to her, mostly because she did not hear it in an official letter by Arnold or Dr. Eicher, she moved to comfort the woman.

"Please do not be so stressed, dear. I'm sure there was reasoning behind this execution of power. He will most definitely land on his feet somewhere as a better fit to that institution."

"It is not him I am so worried about!" she exclaimed in earnest. "I have now been awarded the task of taking over for him for the rest of the fiscal year. How am I to juggle two positions at once? Ms. Allman, would you be so kind as to brainstorm with me so that I may get things in order and begin to sort out this conundrum?"

Thinking that this was, indeed, a problem that needed attention, for it included an entire division of the paper, she agreed hastily but unwillingly.

Had she, at the very least, brought in her team to discuss this? Perhaps not. That is why she had come to me, Genevieve concluded.

They worked the rest of the day writing, crossing out, and rewriting the odds and ends of the packaging situation until it was time for Genevieve and the officer to part ways. The end of day had finally come for them both. Exhausted, and in poor spirit, Genevieve strolled along the corridors back to the conference room, where it seemed that she would be spending another painstaking period of time planning the next day's movements and schematics late into the night.

That afternoon, before Genevieve had set out upon the second part of her misgivings with the packaging department, Pierre Libois was locked in the conference room, thinking over what he had witnessed earlier that morning.

His subordinate had been removed from office, and he wondered, *Was my fourth-quarter report, incurred losses and all, that I had given to Mr. Esche the reasoning for this occurrence? But of course it was! Business as usual, I'm afraid.*

Another moment had passed, and he pondered again, *If not for the undertaking of this project presented, I probably would have been the one to be let go. After all, I am the highest-ranking official in the production department.*

These types of unanswered questions irritated Pierre all afternoon long. Again and again he figured, at the end of these thought tunnels, that Arnold's proposal was the only thing that had saved him from departing *The Absolute Watch*. How could an individual be so important as to display that type of malice and assert ill-placed responsibility on another that was not ultimately to blame? Arnold, of course. He had chuckled to himself in a cynical manner. Then again, it had been that as a group, his contingency was preserved, and he remained a crucial piece to *The Absolute Watch*.

This circular motion of plausibility continued until, late afternoon, a firm yet interrupting knock was placed upon the conference room door. Gathering himself, for he was slouching in his chair at the head of the table, Pierre stood up stepped over to the door. Turning its handle, expecting a matter of official business, he straightened his figure and stepped aside to reveal Sebastian standing in the doorway.

"Good afternoon, sir." He stepped into the frame of the door to address Mr. Libois. "I have just received two letters, one from Mr. Esche and one from Dr. Eicher."

Anxious as he was, thinking these letters could be in retaliation to his production duties, Pierre hurried the youth inside of the room and presented his hand quickly so that he could receive them.

He wiped an imaginary bead of sweat from his brow and carefully opened Arnold's letter first. It read:

Dr. Eicher,

I trust that everything at *The Absolute Watch* is without blemish. It is a fine paper, is it not? It certainly is. Please let me know simply that all is well. I will now give you an insight into just what I have been up to my first month away from business as usual:

I began by traveling south to the countries that are Continental geographically. I was met at port by a team of doctors, lawyers, and politicians that welcomed myself, as well as other diplomats from our state, graciously on behalf of our Board of Directors of The Commerce and Wealth of England. We then traveled to a local establishment for sustenance and indulged informally about the many cultures and traditions of those who were representing their respective lands. I explained to them about the paper, and they seemed most enthralled that I had so many readers. They encouraged me to give a full account of my journey, and I will not disappoint them! After chatting and dining, I took a tour of the local museums, and I was particularly in awe at the number of Medieval paintings and statues that projected an aura of power and prominence. They explained that carrying on the legacy of their fathers was paramount. Can we not resonate with these noble leaders? After all, if we forget our past, are we not doomed to repeat those failures in the future? After touring the many halls of ancient runes and parchments, we were brought to the largest masonry erections in the capital cities for a meeting with all the presidents in the numerous regions of each state. Many topics were discussed, such as economics, environmental protection, government, social issues, and energy. The main goal of these talks was to instill a certain kind of fraternity among our neighbors; one that could be based on similarities would surely bolster the survival of our collective ideals. Uniformity was perhaps the most pivotal topic discussed. After each of these briefings, I was approached by a few representatives of the conference and was urged to speak. They claimed that I was highly regarded by many, as my paper had been circulated among them, and I was not so keen on the idea at first. However, after a few nods from the galleries, I began to gain a certain confidence in their credence. I took the stage and gave rhetoric to one of the only things I am truly familiar with—business. After explaining briefly of the paper, the topics it discussed, and its successes, a roar of applause unironically followed, and I had begun shaking hands with everyone in the room. Journalists were clamoring to get interviews, and I was truly overwhelmed by it all, but only now do I truly believe that I had gotten through to the general public with a few simple words. After this experience, I am filled with conviction. I have decided on my own behalf that I will be running for the highest office in England's government once I return. This proclamation is unshakable, and I am confident this will be easily attained.

Now, Dr. Eicher, I would like you to announce this in the paper so I may start gaining ground on the opinions of those who read it in Downington. A small article is to be constructed once it has been delivered to you. I will pen it myself. Until then, no other interfering action is to be taken. Please follow this request exactly.

Sincerely,

Arnold Esche

After finishing at the bottom where Arnold's signature had been stamped, Pierre lowered the piece of parchment and noticed that his point man was standing attentively, waiting to be instructed. Mr. Libois motioned that he was about to read the second letter given him privately, and the youth stood down immediately.

After reading the few lines that were written, explaining Dr. Eicher's impending absence, he looked up once again, speaking this time, "Thank you, Sebastian, that is all."

Obviously disappointed that the information he had delivered was not shared with him, he nonetheless bowed out of the conference room.

Pierre moved to the seat at the head of the conference table and collapsed into it, his thoughts heavy, drinking in what he had just witnessed through his pupils.

Arnold is certainly moving away from The Absolute Watch *indefinitely. Dr. Eicher will no longer prove disruptive now, and I am free to control the paper's direction.*

He began constructing replies to both men in attempts to set his endeavor in motion.

How will the readers, especially those who are Downington residents, react to this announcement? Genevieve. She was the only person who continued to stand in his path.

Ironically, just as he thought of the latter, Genevieve Allman had pushed her way through the door to the main conference room holding a large stack of papers she was sure to begin organizing. Not immediately noticing Pierre Libois, she slammed them onto the conference table and let out a heaving sigh. As she looked up, surprised as she was, the two made eye contact.

"Good afternoon." Pierre was at a loss for any other phrase.

Though she thought, *There is surely nothing good about it,* she returned the same formal greeting. She noted that he was making notes of a few things and asked him, "Are you here completing some work?"

"That certainly would make two of us."

Genevieve started sorting out the memos and sheets of numbers she had in her arms. There was a tense silence between them, and they stole a few unnoticed glances at each other. Sifting through her documents, she noticed a pamphlet toward the bottom of the heap. Indeed, it was none other than Pierre's "Common Practice." She, again, looked up at Pierre, although he was paying attention only to his letters, and thought dreadfully of her father. Here they were, she and Pierre working as figureheads at this business, and surely, they were both equally responsible for its overall successes and failures.

However, she acknowledged that now the weight she was carrying was immensely greater than his, for she had not seen him all day while she was constantly fixing others' mistakes. This was surely where they differed. Remembering what she had written in her own copy of the pamphlet, she pulled from her pocket a felt pen and scrawled the same words—"Similarities" and "Differences"—on each side respectfully.

After she had completed her paperwork, she strode over to where Mr. Libois was sitting—his head in his hands, attempting to muster formalities to send to his intendeds.

She cleared her throat and looked at him reproachfully. "I think you should take a look at this so you can decide exactly what type of man you are attempting to become in the grand scheme of this paper." Without another word, she took her things and was off.

Startled by the sudden actions of his coworker, he straightened himself up and took the pamphlet in his hands to reveal what Genevieve had written inside.

Upon seeing these two words, he thought, *Poor girl, it seems that simplicity is something that is not in her repertoire.*

6

On the evening that Joanne Freeman sent her driver, Edward Montclair, to deliver her requests, Dr. Eicher had hardly been able to sleep. He concocted scenarios of the two of them in each other's company and began imagined conversations he believed they would have together. When he was able to shut his eyes, it came in fifteen-minute intervals of pure darkness, and this lasted up until the next afternoon. Finally, being able to pry himself out of his bed, he dressed in his most striking attire and stood for some time in front of a mirror he had in his bedroom. He hardly recognized the man standing before him, although he had thought this to make sense because he surely did not feel like himself.

He waited in the foyer for his driver to proceed to Joanne's estate, whom he had instructed, around dawn, to be present in the late afternoon. As the conveyance had pulled around the corner of houses to Dr. Eicher's residence, he felt a keen sense of impending excitement. He did his best

105

not to be without his balance as he closed the door behind him and made way for the carriage.

"Good day, Francis!" the doctor spouted.

Francis Thompson had been Dr. Eicher's driver and confidant since he had been an employee of *The Absolute Watch* at its inception. He was of local stock and had shown the doctor around Downington and surrounding districts to further familiarize him with its population as well as to show him the latest trends of food, fashion, and entertainment.

Noticing Dr. Eicher's linens, he proclaimed, "You are meeting someone of great importance, I see?"

"Someone of the greatest importance. A client to whom I've been entrusted. We will be traveling west on the main drag to the countryside, and I will direct you as such."

"Of course, sir."

As they made their way about the cobblestone in the direction of Joanne's residence, the doctor had broken out into a dreamlike state as he watched the scenery pass through the rear window of the transport. As they moved from the boundaries of Downington into its outskirts, fields of healthy winter wheat were powdered with snow and contained the barren remnants of the previous summer's harvest. In the sky, there were clouds that hung low and hovered over them, following them in their wake. Surely, more snowfall was imminent. However, these circumstances of weather did nothing to dampen the hopeful spirits of the doctor as they moved closer and closer to their destination.

"You may accompany me at our location until it is time for us to part. Is that something you can accomplish for me?"

"Indeed, I can sir."

"Wonderful, I shan't be too long. This is merely being treated as an appointment."

The doctor thought it best to keep his intentions to himself to come to private convictions not influenced by external intrusions. Along they went for an hour, passing over paths of sticky mud and tiny knolls, until they reached an iron gate that was fastened with a large *F* in the middle of it. Two guards awaited their official announcement. As they approached the cart on either side, Dr. Eicher stepped out and bowed to them.

"I am here on behalf of a patient. One Joanne Freeman is awaiting my arrival."

Nodding in unison, one of the guards turned a key he had pulled from the innards of his uniform and pushed open the wrought fortification.

Up a beaten path where snow stood in mounds on either side, Dr. Eicher and Francis Thompson stood at the entrance of the estate. Dr. Eicher had motioned for Francis to place a knock on the door, and as he did so, a maid had opened it for them instantaneously. After bowing politely and stating their purpose once again, they were led into the main sitting room. It was lined with fancies of the most expensive kind. The upholstery was made of purple satin and silk, signifying royalty, and all the trimmings were lined with gold. Francis looked about as though it was all a gaudy facade, but Dr. Eicher was taken in by the splendor. His abode was by no means modest; however, the detail was not as extensively planned out.

They waited for about half an hour, chatting about the eventual journey home and of the prospect of living in such a provincial area when, at last, they were greeted by Edward Montclair.

"Good evening, gentlemen. I hope you have not been waiting too long?"

The pair of them both exclaimed that any length of time was worth waiting for a formal reception.

"Excellent. Dr. Eicher, Joanne will be another moment or two in her private quarters. If you do not mind, she would like you to be moved into the lounge area."

Only too willing to comply, both guests were led to a room three times larger than the one in which they had just been waiting. Here, there were two young men seated at a table with piles of books stacked next to them. One of the young men raised their heads imploringly and was perplexed to see the trio, but the other had quelled his curiosity and was convinced to refocus on whatever it was he was orchestrating.

"You must be an associate of Dr. Eicher?" Edward had addressed Francis.

"Oh yes, I am his personal driver."

"And I, Joanne's! What say we move to the billiard room for a drink so we may let the scheduled pair get on with their business?"

After nodding in approval, the two drivers made their way out of the lounge, and Dr. Eicher was left to sit on a large, comfortable sofa. He noticed the hundreds of books aligned on the far wall and wondered if the two youths were occupied with educational undertakings. After around a quarter of an hour, Dr. Eicher began to pace freely about the room. The doctor's heart skipped a beat when he noticed her enter soon after. Joanne Freeman had appeared through a tiny door juxtaposed to the mountain of books. She too was dressed just as lavishly as he had been.

"Doctor!" she exclaimed and quickly made her way across the room to welcome him.

After removing herself from him, which he truly wished she hadn't, she made a formal introduction.

"Erich, I hope these two here haven't been a bother to you! This is my young relation, Peter."

The boy gave a welcoming, genuine smile.

"To his immediate right is his tutor, Henry."

The latter gave a cold, informal acknowledgment.

"Now, shall we proceed to my quarters?"

Knowing this was a rhetorical question, Erich and Joanne had left the other pair to themselves. After making their way about the maze that was her dwelling, they ended the labyrinth on the top-most floor and entered a room that had its four walls neatly painted flamingo.

Sitting down upon her bedspread and staring her directly in her pupils, Dr. Eicher noticed that Joanne became a contrast, duller color to their surroundings.

"My dear, why have you become so sullen?" He was most genuinely concerned.

"That is something that I am not exactly sure of." Her reply enacted the doctor's patient-study mentality.

"Please let me know of the events that have occurred to you lately. Surely, we will find something that has been producing your current state."

Joanne openly pondered the past few days' occurrences. After drawing a few heaving breaths, she began. As she started her lament, the doctor began to beam longingly at her. He caught such phrases as "my father" and "roaming about the grounds," but for the most part, his ears did not seem to take in anything specifically. Transfixed as he was, and as droningly as she spoke, Joanne seemed to be inching ever closer to Dr. Eicher. Eventually, as her speech began to slow, they were both now so near each other that only breath was being drawn from both persons. In another instant, their faces were as close as they ever could be. As Joanne leaned back cautiously, the doctor blushed a shade that matched the walls. Suddenly he sprang to life with words of the sincerest nature.

"My dear, the reason you have been experiencing such lapses in your happiness is that you need to grasp the physicality of life. You are shut up here in your confinements, and you need to act outside of comfort. New experiences and thrills only await those that seek their accomplishment."

She too shone a different palette. "Oh, Erich, I am only too certain that you are right! Walking about my residence and brooding upon my father has thrown me into a state of trouble. This must be why I am so aggrieved."

Feeling satisfied that this solution would dispel her worry, she thanked him enthusiastically.

"I must write to my father and explain that I wish to take no part in his affairs. Erich, would you mind seeing yourself out? I have so much to consider!"

Agreeably he bowed low and swept from her bedroom. Satisfaction rushed through the doctor much as an avalanche would speed down a mountainside. He had obtained the level of gratification he'd been longing to reach, although he was no closer to establishing a topic on which to write for Arnold's task.

Moving along the winding staircases and corridors, feeling lighter than physical matter, he again reached the lounge area where the two youths had been seated. It was no longer occupied, but books lay open on the table. Still feeling charged, with a stomach for curiosity, the doctor examined them. They were about mathematics, but to his astonishment, they contained functions and equations that were inclined to the basic elementary level.

Just then, as he turned on the spot, Henry appeared. Quite startled, seeing as how the boy appeared almost out of nowhere, Dr. Eicher excused himself and scurried around him.

The youth called after him, "You are a doctor, are you not?"

Erich turned around and answered him respectfully.

Henry approached the doctor and met him face-to-face. Now directly in view of the youth, Dr. Eicher noticed the boy was unusually effeminate.

"Joanne has not stopped raving about you, and I am curious to know if you would consider taking myself up as a patient?"

The doctor explained hurriedly that he was extremely occupied and did not have time to entertain the mind of a child, but Henry pulled out a rolled piece of parchment tied together with string. Looking from the paper and back down to Henry, the doctor noticed painfully that the child's protuberant eyes were on the verge of overflowing with tears. They looked as though they were about to burst.

"Please just read this and tell me what you think the next time you come around," Henry pleaded. Moving quickly from his position, the boy disappeared behind the wall of the leather-bound texts.

Simultaneously, the two drivers appeared through a separate door at the far end of the sitting room, laughing raucously and doubling over with laughter until they noticed Dr. Eicher and steadied themselves gracefully.

"Mr. Montclair is an absolute riot, Doctor. Please tell my companion about that dreadful street performance you saw in town not a day ago!" Francis Thompson was on the verge of tears.

As Edward Montclair gave a brief summary of dancing gypsies, the doctor pretended to take interest but was instead focused on leaving the estate.

As conversation quelled, Erich and Francis said their goodbyes to Mr. Montclair and made their way to their carriage parked at the bottom of the grassy hill and next to the front gate. Still chatting about his encounter in the billiard room, Francis opened the convoy so that the doctor could step inside.

Safely secure, and now out of reach of the unwanted attention, the doctor unraveled the note given to him by the young tutor.

It read:

> People are really —— funny to me. I don't trust a single one of them, not even myself. Nothing but self-interest and pleasure-loving nonsense. We don't deserve to

grace this planet any longer if we keep this "anything is possible" mentality. We need to set strict limits for ourselves simply because we're the only things standing in our own way. We are absolutely "no good" in every sense of the phrase. We continually scheme and plot our way into our own sense of security, claiming that it can help others even by the slimmest of margins, and if you don't think that's the most —— thing in the world, you're probably one of the worst individuals who go about their petty existence every day thinking, "I'm special, and I will change the world and myself for the better."

For the past week, growing ever so sick of life on a speeding vessel, Archibald Cunnings had been keeping a close eye on the man in the black overcoat. For one fact, he had never seen him during the day. This was quite odd for an employee that serviced cars full of paying customers who only slept at nighttime. However, the second day on which Mr. Cunnings had witnessed his suspect's doings, the man entered the first-class section from the rear covered in soot.

He must be a hardworking handyman fortifying the engine and other necessary extensions of the train's operation, Mr. Cunnings concluded.

But once again, when Archibald Cunnings took to the dining car in the evening, he saw the same haggard-looking gentleman guzzling a glass of straight, ungarnished vodka. Archibald was astonished that such an important man was getting incomprehensively inebriated in successive nights. After witnessing the man getting hauled off violently by the same two coworkers, Archibald realized that this was a common routine and not merely happenchance. The other passengers seemed to be getting quite used to the act as they did not become aroused nor inquire as to why this man was being dragged up to the front car for engineers.

Interested by this fact and wanting to get to the bottom of this storm of events, the next day Archibald decided to stop the man after he had finished his shift and ask him to have a drink with Archibald, foregoing his usual predinner snooze. The mood was lax in this section of the train, and indeed all the others, apart from Archibald, were cozying up to rest in their respective seats. Just then Archibald heard the back door of the car open, and looking around surreptitiously, the man—who was covered in thick, black residue—stepped through the threshold and made his way down the aisle. Archibald waited until he was halfway down the carpet-laden alley and stepped in front of him to meet him face-to-face. The man stared wide-eyed at him and shook his head disapprovingly.

Ignoring this physical representation of displeasure, Mr. Cunnings asked, "Is it possible for myself to join you for a drink this evening?"

Taken aback by the casualty of his request, the man merely muttered, "I do not want any trouble."

At this response, Archibald let the man pass without further incident. Though not satisfied, and gripped with a certain lack of deterrence, he proclaimed to himself that he would wait for him in the dining car. Making his way to the exit of the first class and into the entrance of the said car, Archibald sat in the exact same booth that the man seemed particularly fond of and waited patiently. He noticed the bartender stealing a look at him, but from their previous encounters, as Archibald never ordered a drink, the bartender left him to his own devices. About a half hour passed, and Archibald sat unflinching, somehow obsessed with the idea that he should get an explanation out of this stranger.

As the said stranger arrived, Mr. Cunnings slid lower in his seat so as not to be seen. He heard the man ask the bartender for a large glass of his usual order and counted his footsteps as he neared. Collapsing into the seat across from Archibald, the man put the glass to his lips but stopped immediately, horrified. He eyed Archibald, and putting the drink down slowly without breaking eye contact, the two men sat in silence.

"Please leave me be. I want to be alone."

"I just wondered if I could trouble you for a few questions?"

"What for?" the man asked suspiciously, looking more and more afraid.

Archibald had not even answered this question for himself. He thought that maybe genuine interest would be key, and so he replied, "Curiosity about your actions on the train. I don't know why someone who works for this rail line would be able to act in such a manner as yourself, not to mention get away with it. Surely, you'd have been fired for your conduct if there were not some special exceptions in place?"

The man started to look a bit uneasy and shameful at these correct observations.

"Please do not think I am judging your character," Archibald assured him. "Again, I am merely inquiring because I am genuinely curious."

The man looked around and, noticing even the bartender had left the room to restock a few items, breathed a heavy sigh.

"Although I believe your claims of interest, you should be judging my character, for I am not technically employed with this international rail line." He stared deeply into the clear liquid. "I have been sent here to shovel coal to serve as a punishment. I am drinking so heavily because I wish to pass the time."

Archibald began to berate himself for having even attempted to get a confession from the individual.

"My name is Georgy, as I am sure you had wondered that as well."

"Archibald Cunnings."

The two men shook hands. Archibald now wanted to know even more, yet he was hesitant to ask because of how the proceeding conversation had already transpired.

He stood up and was about to give a formal "au revoir" when Georgy stammered, "Please sit down. It would be nice to have some company. After all, it has been a tiresome week for me."

Pleased that Georgy had given Archibald a chance to delve deeper into his inquiry, Mr. Cunnings promised to have just one lager beer with him as they conversed about informal topics such as the landscape of the countryside and the fancies that were strewn about in the cities of his native country. However, not pausing after one drink, Georgy began to become inebriated at a steady pace after his second and third glasses of vodka. Understanding that he would not be competent for much longer, Mr. Cunnings began to ease into much more personal inquiries.

"Georgy, the first time I had noticed you in this dining car, you were babbling about in your native Russian tongue. What do you think you were saying exactly?"

He looked up with a hazy gloss in his eyes, for now he was feeling the effects of the drink.

"Oh, I don't know. Could have been a folk song, or I could have been reciting lines from my favorite poet or writer."

"But you were not speaking out loud, you see. You were hunched over the booth, whispering something to someone. It appears you were pleading with someone. Was it an officer perhaps? Or a government official?" Archibald remembered Georgy told him he was not on board by choice.

At this presumption, the latter began to stare into space with blankness etched into his face. Archibald was thinking he was about to retort or simply refuse to accept the plausibility of the question, but Georgy began.

"What I am about to reveal to you pains me deeply, for it is a most personal and dire matter . . . When I was a boy, growing up in the second-largest city in my country— Petroshov, formerly our capital—I was a member of the highest class of bourgeois society. I attended plays and balls with my family and was raised to believe in our monarchy. Raised to believe that was the ideal way of governing and protecting our people. Of course, only being exposed to this had left me blind to the fact that many of these same citizens were suffering terribly.

"One day in the dead of winter, on my way to a prodigious institution for young gentlemen, I passed a beggar woman who had two babes at her breast. She was rocking them fiercely to stop them from crying, although their stomachs were probably as raw as their tiny, frost-bitten hands. When I asked my mother, accompanying me, if there was anything we could do for them, she replied, 'But we are doing all we can! We afford them allowance for the shelter so they can have something to eat. We donate our old clothes so that they may have something to wear!'

"However, I was not thoroughly convinced. That woman had hardly any clothes to wear, and their three chapped mouths were certainly void of any sustenance. Putting that scene out of my mind for years to come, I grew up wishing and hoping that all the people of my native land would never have to suffer. Even if that meant a select few had to be sacrificed at the hands of a new dawn.

"When I was enrolled in university, I could hardly wait to start making a difference. Now of legal age, my classmates and peers were so deeply involved in politics and social issues that I felt compelled to join the many scholarly activities and clubs that debated these subjects. Even though I was severely uninformed in my youth, I clung to anything that would cement my place among them. I wanted to feel as though I belonged, whatever the cost. 'Revolution' sprang up about a hundred thousand times, rattling about in my consciousness. That ideology seemed to be the consensus, although all understood the damage that could be inflicted to proper establishment and order.

"However, one figurehead stood out among them all, due to most students becoming captivated by her good-natured spirit and empathy. She was Katernova. She preached the likes of democracy, a method in which all might have an equal voice. She would stand on her soapbox and list the wrongs of monarchy, and to her astonishment, we all listened with great earnestness and enthusiasm. A protest was arranged to walk the streets in the center of the city, peacefully organized, and end up on the steps of the seat of government. She had chosen me and another colleague of mine, Sergey Mikhailovich, to accompany her because she valued our enlightened points of view that we had relayed to our philosophical discussions.

"It was a gloomy afternoon, and bitterly cold. We amassed a much larger group than we had intended, previously posting notes upon the university information board, and stood huddled together a few hundred strong. We began our march slowly, somehow gaining courage and purpose as the righteousness swelled in our chests. Many faces of curious onlookers lined the sidewalks of the main roads, particularly those who lived above the shops, poking their heads out to see what all the ruckus was about. When we finally reached the steps of the seated government, there were armed guards at the gate. Standing at attention with their rifles at their sides, we concluded that they were only there to restore order if misconduct broke out. To sharpened young minds, this was completely understandable.

"Katernova climbed the steps to what seemed like a tidal wave of cheers. We were all bellowing our wishes of change, but unfortunately, that is exactly what we were given. Stopping to draw breath, just when the crowd's yells were temporarily at rest, a flaming cocktail was tossed over my head and landed with a shattering crash upon the steps. Instantly, Katernova's linens caught fire, and she dropped where she stood, attempting to put out the flame. Gasps and screams rocked the population while others were turning round and scrambling madly to attempt to find the individual who had performed the wretched deed. The guards left their post and made their way into the human sea, but it was much too loud to shout them into calm. The mass of bodies dispersed in seconds, and no culprit was held accountable . . .

"The next day, we arrived in hospital to comfort Katernova, but to no avail. Her face and body had been badly burned. She was so immobile that even attempting to shed a tear would have riddled her whole body in hurt. The doctor on duty had told us that she would be disfigured and that her speech could possibly be damaged beyond repair. She motioned me over with her unburnt right hand, and I leaned ever so close to her. She croaked, 'Do not let this die. Please. Carry on in my memory. I will never be able to speak again. I appoint Sergey

Mikhailovich at its head and you as his deputy.' She then fell into a deep sleep.

"I immediately rushed out of the emergency center to the mass of others waiting outside. I grabbed Sergey Mikhailovich and breathed to him her request. He nodded mournfully and willingly agreed to take up the post. It would prove to be the worst mistake that anyone could have made. For after this incident, our group of impressionable students was caught up, once again, in revolutionary tactics. Sergey Mikhailovich kept me on as his deputy and promised we would have our place in the sun if I kept his confidence. I was determined, for Katernova, but I always carried a few knots in my stomach.

"Sergey Mikhailovich gave terrible orders and shouted at our members as though they were incompetent children. Never in my life had I been reduced to such stature. I knew what was happening could never produce the results we so ignorantly dreamed of, but it was not so damaging for myself as I was a confidant.

"Weeks later, Katernova died suddenly in her sleep. This seemed most unusual, because internally she was not all that wounded besides her vocal cords. After anticipated medical examinations, the toxicology report revealed it was poison. Everyone wailed and screamed at her funeral, and I, especially, thought this would be a great cause for martyrdom and proper change. But, yet again, it turned out for the worst. At the luncheon and life celebration, Sergey

Mikhailovich told me in secret that it was, in fact, he who had snuffed out the life of Katernova once and for all. He told me that she had begun speaking out against him in print and that because she was out of the public eye, it mattered not that she had gone. I asked if it was he, too, who threw the flaming cocktail at her in the first incident, but he did not answer me. The question was rhetorical.

"At the end of that afternoon, he pulled me aside at our party headquarters and told me, 'Men are inherently weak, and women are inherently strong. If we do not seek to cover up this weakness, then we will forever be overshadowed by them.' These words I believed to be true and ironclad. Not because it was Sergey Mikhailovich that spoke to me, but because I understood the resilience and resolution that Katernova possessed. There was something about her being that I could not explain. An air of confidence and elegance that would have stopped anyone of capable intelligence in their tracks.

"As our political prowess grew, so did the riches and outside contributions did begin to flow like an open water gate to our party. We began to become involved in business, and expansion was imminent. After we had democratically won seats in government—I am still ignorant of the legitimacy—positions were assigned to close relations and trusted cronies we had long-standing relationships with. This surrounded us with an even greater lust for power. We had distributed these riches among citizens in welfare programs but only sparingly. Most of the wealth was concentrated at the lowest percentile, and I am ashamed to say, I accepted plenty of spoils in my tenure. I was incontrovertibly stupider than I had been in the past.

"On one of my daily perambulations, I passed a man crawling on his hands and knees in the waning months of the summer looking rather like a skeleton that would burst into dust at the slightest touch. I was foolish enough to ask him if he needed my help. He gathered an astounding amount of courage and scoffed, 'I'd rather die poor and lifeless returning to the dirt of this earth than be rich and lively, thinking I was past the heavens and miles above it.' He died there on the spot, and my shame had brought me, too, on my hands and knees, embracing this insentient figure.

"I carried his body to the local grave site and dug into the earth with my bare hands, covering him with it and planting his remains. When I finished, I vowed to stand up to Sergey Mikhailovich and reverse my position. This was to be the greatest mistake I had ever made in my life. I told Sergey Mikhailovich about the deceased man and circled back to all the wrongs he had personally befallen upon us. He listened intently and agreed that his path had been sketchy and that he wished to resolve his wrongdoings. Sergey Mikhailovich asked me to board a train to our neighboring countries and take note of their governments so that we could bring our own to reform. Firmly dedicated to my mission as I was, and even more willing as a public servant, I never dreamed of being so blind as to trust the man who had spun so many lives out of control. I am more than ashamed of it!

"When I reached the final stop of my journey, as I tried to leave the train, I was met by policemen from our country and was told that I could not leave the train, and if I attempted to leave, or if I attempted to escape and not be counted as present, there was a large reward for my capture and imprisonment in an asylum. Dumbfounded, I thought about exactly what this situation entailed and realized that I was at the mercy of my former colleagues who no longer had affection for me. I attempted to write to many of them, but all my letters were shredded or did not pass a single willing eye.

"Soon, a division of policemen were assigned to watch the trains on which I was aboard for fear that I may find some way out of this predicament. Shoveling coal is now my forced occupation, for it is free labor and keeps the trains running on schedule. This is perhaps a nod from Sergey Mikhailovich himself because I received a letter at the beginning of this week, proclaiming, 'This is your indubitable service to our country,' and the letter had not been signed.

"Although I am trapped here, hopefully not for the rest of my days, I still have all the amenities of a working individual. I attempt to move along here unnoticed, drinking the very spirit that I wish to become. In a sort of cold comfort, I can now slightly relate to the plight of the man I saw crawling in the street because, although I am not starving or close to death, I hold no possession and am free to be left to my own device on this earth for the minuscule amount of time I am allotted on it, as horrible as that may sound to you."

Archibald was simply horror-struck. This openness and free speech were not what he expected, and he began fumbling in his mind for his own explanations. He instantly thought of Arnold and how he, Archibald, might be running into the same type of barriers that were attempting to warn him. On the other hand, Archibald honestly believed Mr. Esche had no plans of running for political office, for his business endeavors were so successful, and Georgy was obviously insane, to be approving of his captivity. It was pure Stockholm syndrome! He was performing Olympics of neural connections to satisfy his own ironic detest for freedom.

Just as Georgy was attempting to down his sixth glass of vodka, the two employees who had carried him off numerous times slid back the entrance to the dining car.

"Please, gentlemen! Do not take this man away again! He is sick!"

But Archibald's pleas were ignored, and the men grabbed the now-limp drunkard by the arms and tore him away from the booth.

"Why, please, just tell me why you will not oblige!"

"Because this is what we are paid to do," was the definitive, tired reply.

The gentlemen proceeded to return Georgy to the front car for engineers, as the latter fell into a silent stupor.

7

Returning to *The Absolute Watch*, after being convinced herself that she would no longer stand to be the only employee performing necessary tasks, Genevieve was determined to smooth out the paper's kinks so that the departments' extensions could work seamlessly on their own. She arrived earlier than usual, beating Pierre Libois by minutes. That morning she began writing letters to all the department heads demanding that they give her a detailed plan of each department's infrastructure—how decisions were made and who would be taking the responsibility. Feeling satisfied with her finished product, she personally dropped off a letter on their respective desks.

She then made her way to the conference room and found Pierre there sitting alone. Without saying a word, she promptly closed the door.

He probably didn't even notice me, she thought. *He doesn't notice a single thing that goes on in this place. He and Dr. Eicher must be two of the most useless executives that*

I have had the displeasure to come across at The Absolute Watch.

As she entertained this notion, she realized that the doctor was nowhere to be seen.

Lost in his own thoughts at home, he must be! They are both so enthralled with this seemingly insignificant task that they are failing to properly prepare for its takeover.

She had come to such terms that it would be her that would stand as champion in the face of Arnold's permanent absence. To her, the harvest was ripe for the reaping. As she made her way to the various departments later that morning to speak with its heads on operational plans, she passed Sebastian in the hall. The latter was pacing quickly toward the conference room, for another letter addressed to Dr. Eicher was delivered to *The Absolute Watch*. Steadying himself, Sebastian rapped on the large wooden door and was called in by Pierre.

Pierre was still reading Arnold's previous letter, attempting to gain insight on what his next move epitomized. As he looked up and saw Sebastian, he knew that the very letter he was waiting for had arrived. This time, Sebastian looked proud as he was sure to finally be given insight on what was to be put into action regarding Pierre's project. Pierre, too, looked as though this would finally be the answer he was expecting, for he had not yet published Arnold's previous writing, although he was instructed to do so.

Sebastian motioned forward and placed the letter in Mr. Libois's open palm. Pierre tore the letter open at its folded edge and read to himself:

Dr. Eicher,

Enclosed in this letter is the second piece of writing that I ask you to publish. Please do so in earnest because this very article will be the crown jewel of my agenda for *The Absolute Watch* and my newfound political ambition. After meeting with our trusted allies, I was encouraged to travel to lands further east and south of the conference. These destinations are completely foreign to me, so much so that I needed linguists and historical guides to accompany me. I was warned that they differ greatly in all walks of life, and at first, I was keen to the idea that they possessed qualities the likes of our own kith and kin and government. Unfortunately, I was greatly mistaken. I disliked everything about it. The climate, the people, and most unfortunately for them, their government. They do not understand the delicate balance of power and are constantly war-torn. Though I did not spend a long period of time there, I have made my own private conclusions about them. Now, please publish the article listed below, and send a reply that you have done so.

To the People of Wonderful Downington!

Every citizen inside our borders deserves to know the truth! We, the people, bound together by our birth onto this fertile land, must realize that together no outside entanglements can be allowed to threaten our manifest destiny. Recently, I have been made to travel far and wide across this earth, and although I have read and studied about these foreign settlements, I could not have been more wrong about their objective goals and ambitions. If we do not take advantage of our current situation of capital and capabilities, hardships will befall us. Protection of these items is crucial, and we must align ourselves with the strongest possible entities so that we may not only survive but thrive. There are those who are close to us in proximity that possess identical ideals, and governmental practices must be trusted in order to promote brotherhood and fraternity. In doing so, some people in this world must be excluded for all of us here in our homeland to be included. This is an unshakable conviction that I have recently accepted. Other individuals will suffer at the hands of our doing, but it will only prove to be fruitful for our immediate environment. We shall not fear anyone or anything that stands in our way. We must rise together as one to banish our insecurities for good! This is not a time to think, it is a time to act. Go forth now, and shore up fortifications!

Brief though it was, Pierre could not help but notice that Arnold was now reaching a particular rapture of self-transcendence.

"*This is not a time to think, it is a time to act,*" he read over again. "*Some people in this world must be excluded . . . for others to be included.*"

Surely, he knew that Arnold was not particularly fond of understanding others' woes, for no other man, in his view, could possibly gain intelligence from them, but it was incontrovertibly clear what Arnold was trying to accomplish.

Pondering the outcome of publishing this writing, Mr. Libois had again, much like before, noticed Sebastian standing in front of him, eager and awaiting a command. This second piece of Arnold's writing was surely more controversial than the first. Was it necessary to break the news of his political ambition when this most recent piece of writing explained it all so triumphantly? Surely, when the general public got ahold of the paper with this emblazoned headline, there would be a greater groundbreaking than if it stood alone without the pretense of an announced candidacy.

Pierre thought this over, rapidly staring at the letter. He had no choice but to decide on whether to publish both of Arnold's requests. Arnold would surely find out if neither had been put to page. Mr. Libois decided to consult Sebastian this time, for the youth had now been shuffling around in his peripheral vision.

Looking up, he said, "Sebastian." He led on in a subtle tone, "Mr. Esche wishes to have this piece of writing published in the next edition of the paper and put on its front page. Could you please deliver it to the editing room and proclaim that the decision came directly from himself and Dr. Eicher?"

Darting his eyes to meet Mr. Libois, he proclaimed, "But of course, sir! I have plenty of close colleagues to whom I can give it to that will publish it unquestioningly."

Sebastian nearly snatched the paper out of Pierre's hands as he reached out an arm to surrender it into the former's possession. Sebastian then bowed himself out of the conference room, and his footsteps fell heavily outside in the hallway. Pierre spun around and made his way to the head chair at the large wooden table in the middle of the room.

The deed is done then, he assured himself.

Although Pierre and Arnold were not close regarding their personal goals and endeavors, it was now clear that they had indefinitely been intertwined. Arnold was giving up his control of *The Absolute Watch*. This much was certain. Erich Eicher and Archibald Cunnings were in no position now to physically stop any order that Pierre decided to carry out. Genevieve was present the entire time, but she was much too busy and troubled with the paper's operation that she certainly was not paying him any mind. He had a faithful comrade in Sebastian who would help him accomplish his aspirations. It seemed that Pierre's wishes were being granted much too easily and without the slightest case of friction. All these people—these players, most importantly—were in Pierre's calculation. Their formulation was exactly as he expected them to be.

Just as Pierre began to gain solace in this time of scattered thought, a knock befell the door to the conference room.

"Come in," Pierre called. He was broken from his current train of thought.

It was Sebastian again, and a look of worry was plastered across his face.

"Sir, I have some news."

Sitting up straight and folding his hands upon the table in earnest, feeling that it could not be of the positive nature, Pierre asked him what news he had to bring.

"The heads of all the departments—accounting, human resources, and production and packaging—would like to call a meeting together with you and Dr. Eicher. They are concerned about the impact Arnold's writing will have on *The Absolute Watch*'s readership. They ask for both of your words in expediency."

A lurch occurred within Pierre's stomach. Settling himself, he thanked Sebastian for bringing him this vital information and motioned him out of the conference room. A new task had been placed at the feet of Mr. Libois, and this time especially, his untruthfulness was going to have to be inflated to the point to which it could not be overlooked. He began to feel sickly and made to stand so as his frame would not be crunched in an awkward position. He left the conference room, half noticing and half unknowing, and began to walk down the hall to the lavatory.

As he reached its entrance, he traveled to the sink, where he turned both handles to produce warm water. He then used his hands to cup some of it and wipe it upon his face. Moving his attention to the mirror in front of him, he stared back at himself. His hands were clutched on either side of the porcelain. His pupils were reflecting the scene of him watching himself as they started to widen.

He began running through the past few days' events and analyzing them accordingly.

The Absolute Watch, Arnold, his competitors, Genevieve, the other employees of the paper, the meeting he was now forced to attend. All these were finally accumulating to the point of inflating and overflowing his consciousness.

Was this the man he wished to become? Did this task mean so much to him as to risk his own personal betterment and reputation?

Arnold was certainly that type of individual. But then again, returning to the topic he had discussed for the presidency of *The Absolute Watch*, it was not the single being that had an effect on others but a committee of them. Pierre sank deeper and deeper into his own reflection. He began to examine all physical aspects of his facial structure. He thought for a split second that he saw his eyes produce a yellowish glint. He bared his teeth, and they too were a slight shade of the same pale color. Snapping back into the silent bathroom, he decided to go down and meet with the other chieftains and speak on behalf of himself and Dr. Eicher. His duty to be the sole possessor of *The Absolute Watch* was not a promise he would be breaking to himself.

As Pierre made his way down through the many hallways and corners of *The Absolute Watch*'s infrastructure, he found it increasingly difficult to convince himself that this meeting would go without difficulty. Dr. Eicher had not been seen or heard from by any other members at the paper for quite a period of time, and this previously opened article could obviously not have sprung up of its own accord.

Finally reaching the level where the main offices were located, he entered the landing and was greeted by a busy-looking female secretary who was filing documents and speaking out loud to herself. As she noticed Mr. Libois from the corner of her vision, he stepped up to her desk so that his frame was directly in front of her. As politely as he could, he stated his purpose. She pointed to a corridor behind her and instructed him to seek its end. Thanking her most genuinely, because she had looked terribly overwhelmed, Pierre strode past her and quickly made his way to the end of the place where she had navigated him.

He approached a door that was slightly opened, and he could hear a few individuals chattering away. Taking a deep and steadying breath, he knocked three times then pushed it open. Sitting at a large wooden table, much like the one in the main conference room where Pierre frequently sat planning his own agenda, were three people locked in conversation.

Here sat the second-level instructors of the business. The managers situated from left to right were as follows: the accounting manager, the human resources manager, and the production and packaging manager. This was Mr. Libois's first formal meeting with them, and although he outranked them in a sense of superiority, they had much more knowledge and skill when it came to the actual tactics of the paper.

As the human resources manager had the final word with the group, discussing a topic unbeknownst to Pierre, they all looked attentively in his direction and became much calmer than they had been when they were in their three-way exchange.

"Greetings, Mr. Libois. Please excuse our babble. I am so very pleased that you have answered our request to come see us on such short notice."

The other two seated at the table nodded in agreement.

Pierre gave a shallow bow, and the woman continued, "It has come to our attention that you had come across a letter written by Arnold himself and that he wished to have it published for the most recent edition of the paper. This is correct, is it not?"

Feeling as though this was more of an accusation than a question, Pierre began to imagine how he would decidedly back up this knowledge. Attempting to procure some time to formulate a thought, he gave a stern, "Yes."

"Well," she continued, "we think that it is simply genius!"

Taken aback by the word *genius*, Mr. Libois was thunderstruck.

"This is certainly a typical tact of Arnold's, the old coot! This false display of hard-line politics is surely to rouse up our readers. Creating this type of storm will produce a debate the likes of which the paper has not seen in years. As you probably have noticed, having access to numerical reports, our last quarter was something of a disappointment. Although our stories and world-class pieces are lauded, there has been nothing to grab the readers' attention, and the three of us agree that Arnold has finally decided to shake things up."

Consuming this statement and grasping the new particulars of the conversation, Pierre breathed a sigh of relief. He agreed, understanding all too well that their counsel was of false pretense.

"Now that we have agreed to make this front-page news," the woman continued, "we must disclose to you the current affairs we have taken up in Arnold's absence."

Pierre nodded and listened on in earnest.

She motioned to the accounting manager for him to speak.

In doing so, he gave a monotone proposal, "We, as figureheads, believe it is our duty to do what is best for this business. Tough decisions must be made, and we are the ones responsible for them. Due to this fact, we must cut fat from areas that are not producing."

He looked at his two other colleagues at the table as they confirmed unanimously.

"We have come up with a plan to fire a good portion of workers in the writing, editing, and production departments. I ran some numbers and analyzed the possibility of being short-staffed in these areas to great avail. This would decrease our workforce significantly, however there would be ample opportunity for those who carry this business. We are proposing a wage increase that would have an effect on the three of us, you, Mr. Cunnings, and Dr. Eicher."

Listening intently, Pierre asked the man to continue.

"This would require conformation from a high-ranking member, and seeing as how Arnold, Archibald, and Erich are not capable of being present at the moment, we wondered if you would approve this in their absence?"

Again, attempting to follow the prose carefully, Pierre realized that he was being asked by his inferiors to make an executive decision. This was exactly the type of indication that he was finally beginning to outflank the others in procuring his place at the top.

He turned his head to either end of the group and affirmed, "Please give me all the necessary paperwork and formulations so that I may review them. Upon this, I will make my final decision and hand you a signed declaration."

After unanimously agreeing that Arnold's writing would make the next available headline, Pierre received the documents from the man of the accounting department. Once again, Pierre bowed and walked back the way he had come in. Passing the secretary and leaving the area of the main offices with a new sense of purpose, Pierre knew he was now ideologically very deep in the syndicate of *The Absolute Watch*.

After the small conference had dissolved, the woman who was head of the combined production and packaging department had left the accounting manager and human resources manager to work out the kinks of their hopefully successful new proposal. She passed the secretary and asked if there was anything she could do to help her, but the latter seemed to be too entrenched in her work to give a direct reply.

As the production and packaging manager left the main area of the offices, she felt it prudent to visit the floor where the paper was constructed into sections and bound together in bundles so that it could be shipped off to various distributors in towns nearby. Finally arriving at the first station where the pulp of the paper was dried and cut, she noticed that the workers were not at their respective posts.

As she moved on to the second phase of the process, the inking and headlining, she observed the same. All the machines were running, but nothing was being churned out. Thinking this was odd, since it was well past lunchtime and their company-wide break had already taken place an hour ago, she made her way to the loading area where the paper was piled into carts to find a gathering of employees in a circle with an individual at their head.

Ms. Allman seemed to be orating to them. The woman was only able to overhear a brief portion of Genevieve's speech before they scattered, heading back to the lines of production that they occupied.

Genevieve spotted the production and packaging manager and came beelining toward her.

"These workers really need to be motivated at least five times a day. Some of them were sitting around and conversing. One gentleman even had his eyes closed, sleeping in an upright position."

The manager, who had minor experience in this field, was not so taken aback as she knew the kind of fate that awaited them. Nonetheless, she understood that Genevieve was of great use to her, having helped her with problem-solving on a few occasions since Arnold Esche and Dr. Eicher had been absent.

She took Genevieve aside, and with an "I-want-to-be-the-one-to-tell-you-and-I-must" sort of look, she began, "My dear girl, there are about to be a few changes here that I think would be of valuation for you to know."

Genevieve looked slightly puzzled.

"We have made a proposal to Pierre Libois about some key firings that we are certain he will accept, and although I know your name is secure in the future of this company, I must admit that you will be missing out on a great portion of its wealth."

Appreciative though she was to know this proprietary information, Genevieve was still perplexed.

Did this woman know about Arnold's handing over of the company?

The manager from production and packaging continued, "We—I mean, the moving parts of this organization—will be amassing the salaries of those who have proven to be useless extensions. I am afraid that the financial aspect of this is not in your favor, for you are not being included in this revamp."

Genevieve began to understand the woman and thought of her poor father. These workers, men and women alike, needed these positions to live. Not only were there plans to deprive them financially, but to outright destroy their livelihood! What would happen to themselves and their families? Ms. Allman was not sure why these questions mattered to her and why they weighed on her so. Although she was not to be out of a job, the proposed situation seemed to be of no concern to herself.

"I would suggest that you pay Mr. Libois a visit and try and procure yourself at least an additional tranche, for soon there will be nothing left but fractions of a fraction!"

The manager of production and packaging finished speaking with Genevieve and, after giving her a small nod of endorsement, began walking back through the production line, putting on a scrupulous face for her eventual unemployed.

After a minute or two of deep processing, Genevieve slowly became hotter and hotter by the moment.

So these people at the top think they can just exclude everyone else without an attempt at help for better character and cause? This reminded her unmistakably of Arnold and his condescending attitude toward her. *He, Mr. Libois, Dr. Eicher, and Mr. Cunnings were undoubtedly playing games with these people's lives just to make a bigger fortune for themselves. I am glad that I have no hand in this!* she thought relieved.

But then she realized that not acting would be much worse than sidelining herself from the eventual outcome of events.

I will speak to Mr. Libois immediately, was her immediate aim.

As Genevieve made her way up to the conference room, where she was sure Pierre would undoubtedly be looking through the aforementioned documents of downsizing, she passed many workers who would, in a few minutes' time, be leaving after another day's labor. She made note of their faces, some defeated and others downright joyful to be leaving.

She pondered, *Employment is surely a necessary mechanical objective for people for quite a few reasons. First being that it keeps them busy, and second that capital could improve people's well-being if handled in the correct measurement of want and need.*

She convinced herself that *The Absolute Watch* should not fire these people because they truly needed it as an entity. This she would need to prove to Pierre Libois.

As she approached the conference room door, she did not knock but opened the door of her own accord.

Unknowingly, and just as she had expected him to be, Pierre was looking over documents in front of him. Genevieve cleared her throat, and Mr. Libois looked up unbothered.

"Please tell me you won't be signing those," she stated in a tone of utter sincerity.

"Not that it is any of your business," he retorted, "but you do not even know what you are talking about."

"You think that I am so ignorant? You think that everything here is confided in secret?"

Pierre looked inquisitively at her.

"I have been alerted of your reckless plan to sign documents that will result in the expulsion of many here at the paper. Do you really want to be the one responsible for this?"

Mr. Libois stood up, naturally moving his chair backward. "Tough decisions must be made for the benefit of those who have the most responsibility. Whether that means protecting some and banishing others is not a matter for those like yourself who only reside on the outskirts of the situation. I have made up my mind, and I will sign."

As he pulled his seat back toward him, he grabbed the ink pen that was in front of him and made a wispy signature appear on a bold, black line at the bottom of one of the pages next to an equally bold letter X and picked it up to show Genevieve that he had signed it.

"I hope you rue this decision forever, it does not have to be like this!"

"On the contrary, Ms. Allman," he proclaimed with conviction, "it has always been like this."

That very evening, Arnold's proclamation had been posted to the front page of the paper. As it made its way through the lines of production, not a single eye curiously met its lettering. From the papermaking station to where the final product was bound together in bundles, no employee was aware that Mr. Esche's words were about to make their way to the general public. Slowly, upon carts and conveyances, it was distributed to local businesses and residencies. As the still after-hours of the evening turned into the soft sky of morning, the population of Downington would be entrenched in a new kind of discussion—one that would test their abilities in understanding the motivations of an unseemly antisocialite.

8

Following his previous encounter with Joanne Freeman, Erich Eicher was finally able to sleep soundly without any kind of interruption whatsoever. He did not toss and turn nor have a preconceived thought in his head. When he awoke in the morning, he was utterly refreshed. He could not remember such an occasion where he had not dwelled upon some sort of passing trouble during his periodical rest. As he lay upon his sheets with his eyes closed, he began to mull over recent events. He saw Ms. Freeman and himself together, lounging about in her room and simply lying next to each other side by side.

He tried to remember what they had discussed when he had made his journey to her estate, but he could not remember. Confirming that it could not have been all that serious, as he was still to be accompanying her to her father's dinner party, he removed himself from his area of comfort and began to dress.

"I must start working on a topic for Arnold," he told himself.

As he made his way downstairs into the foyer, he noticed that his personal driver, Francis Thompson, was stepping down from his conveyance and scurrying up the walkway to his front door. Opening it, to save Francis the displeasure of knocking and possibly waking up his nominal overseer, Dr. Eicher met him at the doorframe with a look of inquiry upon his face.

"Pleasure to see you this early, Francis." With an air of understanding, the doctor let him pass through the threshold and into the foyer. "To what do I owe this unannounced and unscheduled appearance?"

"Please, sir, if you would allow it, or be comfortable with it for that matter," he started, "I would like to revisit the estate of one Joanne Freeman."

A bit taken aback at this request, although the doctor would not mind it at all returning to the place where his interest resided, he felt that he must ask Mr. Thompson why he felt compelled to return.

Answering the doctor, after the said question was put to him, Francis admitted, "I would like to speak with her contemporary, Edward Montclair."

Feeling that this was a satisfactory appeal, for they were both drivers and probably had much in common with each other, Dr. Eicher agreed that they would return this very day to the estate. Elated at the fact that the doctor confirmed this sporadic turn of events, Francis asked for an hour or two so that he might return home to properly prepare for the occasion.

As Dr. Eicher watched him strut back to the carriage, he made his way into the tearoom where his desk stood barren to begin a topic of thought on Joanne. As he had made several attempts before, this one also turned out to be fruitless. Frustrated but not yet deterred, he began to imagine her estate with all its dazzling trimmings. Longingly, he pictured her bedroom where they had ended up during their previous meeting; but, yet again, he found not the slightest notion of interest to write upon. Circling his thoughts for what seemed like a few short moments, Francis Thompson returned, dressed in a fine blue suit and sporting a monocle.

Rolling along the exact path they traveled the first time they made the trip to Joanne Freeman's estate, they saw the suburban area was still riddled with flakes of precipitation. The doctor was now brooding upon Ms. Freeman, partially because he had still not been able to formulate an interesting piece about her and partly because he was not formally invited to visit her. As they approached the wrought iron gates, after about an hour's travel, they made a point to stop and inquire this time if Joanne was inside her place of residence. The guard at the post, who recognized them, explained she had left a few moments earlier to stroll about Downington's bazaar.

Just as Dr. Eicher was ready to apologize to Francis, for it was not proper to enter the home of someone who was not present, the latter exclaimed, "Could you call for Mr. Montclair then perhaps?"

Nodding in agreement, the guard turned the key to the gate, closed it, then proceeded up the hill to the massive structure. Figuring that this was the purpose of their trip initially, the doctor sat patiently until the guard had returned with the beckoned-for Edward Montclair. Surprised to see the duo, although pleased that they had arrived, Mr. Montclair declared them as guests, and the now trio walked up the path to the front door of the building and passed through it.

Once again, they were standing in the purple- and gold-laden sitting area where they had waited a time for Joanne to appear. Explaining his and the doctor's visit, Francis once again had been led away to the billiard room while Dr. Eicher was free to roam around the study. Once he stepped into the large space, a wall of books to his immediate right, he made his way over to the wooden table where Joanne's relation and his tutor had been practicing mathematics. He noticed a very old and tattered binding upon it and turned it thrice in hand. Just then, from the same place Joanne had emerged, beside the wall of books, a young man spotted the doctor and approached him cautiously.

Placing the book back on the table, and forgetting the young tutor's name, Dr. Eicher politely asked him again.

"Henry, sir." After giving his name, Henry eyed the doctor, imploring him to speak before himself letting out, "Well, what did you think?"

Dr. Eicher thought sparingly on this question and replied, "Think about what?"

Henry drew a heavy and exhausting breath. Without a word, he left the study for a minute to retrieve a piece of parchment that was tied in a ribbon of string.

"I made a few copies for myself, and seeing as how you have displaced your previous one, I will lend this alternative to you."

Dismantling the string and rolling out the paper, Dr. Eicher read for a second time:

> People are really —— funny to me. I don't trust a single one of them, not even myself. Nothing but self-interest and pleasure-loving nonsense. We don't deserve to grace this planet any longer if we keep this "anything is possible" mentality. We need to set strict limits for ourselves simply because we're the only things standing in our own way. We are absolutely "no good" in every sense of the phrase. We continually scheme and plot our way into our own sense of security, claiming that it can help others even by the slimmest of margins, and if you don't think that's the most —— thing

in the world, you're probably one of the worst individuals who go about their petty existence every day thinking, "I'm special, and I will change the world and myself for the better."

Slowly coming to the realization that he had read this before, the doctor now remembered the look on the youth's face when he had given this piece of writing to him on the previous occasion that he visited Joanne's estate. Focusing his greatest effort, Dr. Eicher had amassed the notion that this child needed help.

Wanting to be calm in his tone, he began, "I see that you have a great dislike for others. Am I correct in this assumption?"

Henry was stifled in his reply. "On the contrary, I care greatly for my fellow man. I just believe that I understand their motives quite well. As mere human beings, I'm sure they believe the same."

The doctor pressed on, "Please explain to me the meaning of this passage. It seems to be full of negativity that stems from great loathing. I am, as you know, a certified doctor, and this will be a matter of confidentiality."

The youth made his lament, "First of all, I would like to thank you, Doctor, for taking time out of your existence to hear me ramble on about mine. Through many hours of deep mental processing, I have concluded that I do not deserve to exist. What I have written about humanity, the piece that you have just kindly read a second time, would not make any sense if those criticisms did not include myself within them. I have tunneled deep into my conscious and have found that I am becoming despondent to what little good nature I have left. My actions are becoming more and more calculated, making them ever more perverse. This is surely a cynical view, but if I, too, am a part of humanity, does this not mean that others are also capable of feeling the same?" Henry was in a deep, blank stare.

The doctor urged for his continuance by adding, "What defines this humanity to you?"

"As basic objective life-forms, there are divisions in our cells, though organically speaking, we are absolutely identical. Differences in our X and Y chromosomes then separate us into male and female sexes. Although, again, we have been separated by this natural occurrence, we are identical physically, both sporting organs, skin, bones, and limbs. The next difference is within the compound chemicals that have been assigned. Testosterone and estrogen exist in different levels in the two sexes, however together they are similar because they are both produced in each respective sex. The difference of sex that is greater in testosterone is naturally dominant, while the sex that is greater in estrogen is naturally docile. These combinations of differences and similarities are the quagmire of the existence of our species."

"And what produces such a quagmire?"

"The everlasting question of experience, of course. Triumph and trauma are two great polar opposites. If one experiences more triumphs than trauma, they will be subject to positivity and power. If one's experience falls prey to trauma, negativity will be spread wholly upon them, and they will become downtrodden. These constant ups and downs have the power to shape an individual with great ease."

The doctor was still very unsure why this young man was comparing and contrasting such things but let him continue.

"Physical being matched with intangible requiem divides this existence into two very simple planes: objective and subjective. However, I have combined them with other planes that I have come to accept based on a mathematical model I have recently been studying."

Henry motioned the doctor to look at the old, tattered book that was lying on the table. He opened it and removed from its pages a piece of paper folded into quadrants. He unfolded it by its edges and smoothed it out so that the heading was properly placed at the top for the doctor to read. Drawn by hand was a Cartesian coordinate system.

"Here," Henry had pointed to the center of two perpendicular lines, "is the point of origin." He pointed to a "0, 0" upon it. "This is an individual's birth." He motioned left to right on the horizontal line. "This is the X-axis, and it represents the objective plane of existence. Negative to positive respectively." He then did the same vertically but moved his hand up then down. "This is the Y-axis, and it represents the subjective plane. Positive to negative respectfully."

The doctor seemed to be lost in this explanation but let the youth continue.

"And these . . ."—he drew two lines, one from the third quadrant to the first and one from the second quadrant to the fourth—"are the bijective planes. Both lines represent the objective passing into the subjective, the third quadrant into the first, and the subjective passing into the objective, the second quadrant into the fourth. This Z-axis represents two important occurrences in a human's experience and understanding of the world.

"The bijective plane includes the two concepts of aesthetics and metaphysics respectively. Aesthetics represents the line from the third quadrant into the first. This line starts out as a purely negative objective nature and inclines into a purely positive subjective nature. Metaphysics represents the line from the second quadrant into the fourth. This line starts as a balanced negative objective–to–positive subjective ratio and transforms into a balanced positive objective–to–negative subjective ratio."

Seeming to round up and conclude his theory, Henry then drew a circle around the entire coordinate and pronounced, "Last, but certainly the most important, is the T-axis. This axis contains all other axes representing the concept of time. All that happens and what will eventually happen to all newborn people occur within its ring. Anywhere you place a point on this system, there will be a particular event in time and space for an individual that it will fall under, be it triumph or trauma."

Henry was now at a point of utter dilapidation. The veins in his forehead were pulsating, and he was red in the face. Tears were running down his cheekbones, and although he was completely silent, he looked, at least to the doctor, as if he were going to combust. Without another word, Henry left the doctor sitting alone in the study, with the piece of paper and the book lying before the latter.

Dr. Eicher, not wanting to interrupt the youth and cause any more friction, pocketed the piece of paper and put the book back in an empty space on one of the many shelves to complete the collection. After such a display of confusion, the doctor made his way back to the sitting area to wait for Francis.

A half an hour or so later, Francis and Edward Montclair had returned, once again jovially speaking about topics they had discussed. With a bow out from Mr. Montclair, the pair of visitors made their way back down the hill to their conveyance, and once again, Mr. Thompson was raving about Edward Montclair.

Trying with great difficulty to pretend that he was interested, Dr. Eicher became very curious about the nature of the topics Henry had discussed with him. Being a doctor of the mind, he was not so sure that the youth's was working properly, so to speak. Then it hit him. Where he was, who he had been talking with. All of it seemed to make sense. A timeline had occurred so naturally. Dr. Eicher would write about Henry to try and win the presidency of *The Absolute Watch*.

Back on the train to Siberia, Archibald Cunnings played over the conversation he had had with Georgy for the next few days. He pondered how anyone could be so misled about their situation, and although it clearly wasn't his business, he decided that he would try and help this poor man escape his current fate.

He pleaded with the other passengers to gain their assistance in this matter.

However, the man in the large top hat had exclaimed, "Do you really believe such a person could exist in such a way? Clearly, his mind is playing tricks on the old fellow!"

Meanwhile, Mr. Cunnings overheard the woman with the pearl necklace whisper out loud, "You see how drunk he becomes? This is a matter of his own device. I believe he is getting exactly what he deserves."

After this frantic attempt to gather support for Georgy, Archibald thought it best to take this matter into his own hands, to remain the only culprit and not involve any innocent parties—guilty though the rest of them were to turn their back on someone who was clearly in trouble.

As all the passengers were slowly arriving ever closer to their destination, the weather outside along the track was becoming icy and snow-hardened. A few times the train skidded to a halt, and the occupants were told they had to wait a moment for someone to physically clear the train's path so that the cars could carry on along their route. Archibald told himself that this would be an opportune time to help get Georgy off the train. Mr. Cunnings reiterated this plan to himself as houses were now starting to spring up along their path; perhaps someone would be kind enough to take the wretched soul in. He spent a whole day attempting to work out any problems he would face in their getaway plan.

First, he would wait for Georgy to become inebriated; he didn't want him refusing out of fear or confusion. He needed to seize him before his coworkers did, and that gave him a very shallow window of time. He decided it was best to go through the back of the dining car where he knew the kitchen to be; that way they could grab a bit of sustenance to sustain him as he made his way to a nearby village. All things considered, that very evening the plan was put into action.

Archibald started his predinner routine, as usual, being the first to arrive in the dining car out of all the other passengers. There, once again, was Georgy sitting alone; he was whispering to himself once more in his isolation. Archibald strode over, nodding to the bartender, passing him, and making his way to a booth halfway down the dining car. He picked Georgy up by his underarm and stood him up. Georgy had almost dropped his glass of vodka but then steadied his grasp around it. Before he could turn his head to see who had interrupted his invisible conversation, they began walking to the back of the dining car to the kitchen.

As they entered, the smell of soup filled their nostrils, and lucky for Archibald, a bag of bread lay upon one of the countertops. Georgy was now teetering under his own weight as Mr. Cunnings scooped up the loaf and placed it in Georgy's arms. Now heading to the rear of the kitchen, Archibald spotted a disposal chute and next to it an opening for larger objects to be dumped through.

He pushed Georgy into the corner where it resided and told him, "Stay here."

He did not believe that the drunken man heard him, although he was quite occupied, as he was muttering more words in his native tongue to himself. Archibald kept guard for only a moment when the train had skidded to a halt. Realizing this was his moment, he brought Georgy back up to his feet. Mr. Cunnings pried the large opening from its hatch and directed him through it. He watched hopefully as Georgy hobbled down the landing on the side of the train and spun around, spilled glass of vodka and bread in hand.

Now, in the depths of winter, Georgy had started stumbling forward, and just ahead of him lay a row of modest-looking abodes. Feeling that his job had now been completed, Archibald removed himself from the opening and made his way back to the dining car. Being overcome with a new sense of accomplishment, Mr. Cunnings was now clear of mind to retrieve the object that Arnold Esche had asked him to recover. It now fell upon him that he was to be the paper's new chieftain. Attempting to clear his mind of Georgy, he would certainly start making plans for it.

As he walked back into the dining car, he was called over by the bartender. Mildly startled, Archibald approached the man to apologize for his disinterest in a drink. However, the bartender was looking sternly at him. Perplexed, Mr. Cunnings waited for the man to say something.

"Why did you let him go? You had no right in doing so."

Becoming slightly uncomfortable, Archibald knew the barman had found him out. "I was only trying to help him break free of this monstrous routine he had been bound to."

The barman scoffed, and Mr. Cunnings became more and more uneasy.

"Let me tell you something, sir. No matter who you are or whom you encounter, greater things are always at work. Be they calamitous or calming, be they the definition of right or the definition of wrong in whatever dictionary is most fashionable at the time. Everyone has a place in this world in which we live. You may be able to change some things, but the greater picture certainly will not. I just had to dispatch two men to go and catch Georgy because he is a vital piece of the inner workings of this train. Defection cannot be tolerated on any level."

Archibald wondered anxiously if he, too, was about to be punished by the same forces that encircled Georgy.

"You see this here?" The bartender was running his hand along a thin, yellow cable that was running along the back of the wooden counter.

Mr. Cunnings leaned over and acknowledged it.

"This is how those two workers knew to come and retrieve him every single night. I had made it so because Georgy could not stand to be left to his own device. In a controlled environment such as this, he was at least safe. He had freedom to do what he wished after he had contributed his fair share to this railway."

Sensing that Archibald Cunnings was about to interrupt him, he said curtly, "Yes, I know the conditions on which he was placed here. It seems like a very fair situation to me. He had all the amenities of a working-class individual, and it seemed to be working out for him just fine until you decided to throw a wrench into his daily go-about. I'm sure that if the situation was reciprocated, he would definitely attempt to help you as well. However, not everything is fixable. Some events are stagnant because they are better off that way. If you just go around changing any bit of occurrence into an ideal for a better outcome, then nothing would be a solid foundation on which to build."

Archibald had finally been able to get a word in. "But please tell me then, why he is a prisoner? He could do just as well out in the world without having to be stuck on this conveyance!"

"That is merely a risk that someone is just not willing to take. I have my place here. I play my part very well, and for that I have at least a sliver of respect and liberation for myself. Duty in the simplest sense is to be predictable. When a type of blind faith is introduced between two or more individuals, the outcome of the fruits of labor can be quite bountiful. There exists an ever-so-slight advantage in any kind of relationship. The weight may be quite one-sided to the untrained, outside eye, but as long as the two parties are aware of this disproportionate distribution, there will be no conflict of interest or any type of friction that could divide them."

Again, simply horror-struck, Archibald backed away from the man and spouted, "You're mad . . . you're all mad."

Just then, from the rear of the dining car came the two employees who regularly sought to displace Georgy from his drinking spree. In their arms was Georgy, all of them sopping wet and covered in bits of frost.

"Do you know what he whispers to himself when he is in a stupor?" the barman was addressing Archibald, knowing he did not know any bit of Russian. "He is praying that mercy be taken upon him. His past seems to be tearing him away from his present. I know not what he had done or failed to do, but he seems to find solace somewhere at the bottom of a few glasses of liquor. Who am I to take away that tiny piece of comfort from him? I would be overstepping my bounds to think that I had such power. You cannot control another's thoughts or actions, to do so would be as selfish as an act of defiance to one's own morale. If you let others come between what you know and what you think you know, then you will be forced into a state such as he is now." He pointed to the now-limp Georgy whose lips had turned a pale blue. "Take him to his quarters so that he may be dried up and ready for work in the morrow."

The two employees nodded and dragged the lifeless body along, making a stained streak of a line with two footsteps in unison on either side down the carpeted path where, again, heads turned and gave disapproving *tuts*. Georgy was pulled through the sliding door that housed the engineers and slid silently behind it.

Next day, as he awoke in his seat in the first-class rail car, Archibald Cunnings mulled over the events that had occurred the previous night. It had seemed a little more than a dream. He was now convinced that Georgy's situation was utterly foregone. No sense was made by the barman, and yet he now understood what was weighing so heavy on the drunkard's mind. He had explained to him the story of his political endeavors and how the terrible outcome had come to fruition. Mr. Cunnings felt even more sorry for him now, more than ever.

As the morning switched to afternoon, the conductor notified all passengers that they would be arriving in Siberia at its main station in about an hour's time. Archibald's thoughts rerouted to Arnold and *The Absolute Watch*. A brass box. That was what he was meant to recover. However, not a single shred of information more was shared with him by Mr. Esche. Where would he start looking for it? How would he know if it was the correct item? As he gathered his belongings and waited patiently among the others, all of them finally saw the station through the icy windows of the car.

Once it came to a halt, they stood up, juggling their many possessions, and made their way single file to the exit. As Mr. Cunnings's permanence was at the front of the first-class car, he would be one of the last of those to deboard. Peering out onto the platform, Archibald saw the other first-class passengers being greeted by military personnel.

Some sort of business contracting, he concluded.

Just then, as he made his way to the exit, an officer of the said military coalition stepped onto the train. He passed a few stragglers of the car. Archibald guessed correctly that he was the subject of this man's mission. Mr. Cunnings had attempted to help a prisoner of the state escape, and for that he, too, would be imprisoned.

So much for returning to claim my prize, he thought dejectedly.

As he put his hands out to be handcuffed, the officer stopped just in front of him, clicked his heels together, and gave a salute. Up close, through the opening in his long, furred coat, Archibald noticed this man was overwhelmingly decorated. He wore a field-gray uniform that was tended in the most careful way all the way down to his shiny, black boots which matched his jacket, gloves, and fur hat. Thinking this was an odd way to treat a newfound detainee, Archibald put his hands at his sides. The man then dug into the inner pocket of his coat and pulled from it a small bronze box. Mr. Cunnings hesitated but nonetheless reached out to retrieve it from the outstretched palm in front of him.

The officer spoke, "Mr. Archibald Cunnings. My orders are to present you with this second-class medal for special services to our government. It is to be awarded by you to one Mr. Arnold Esche. You will remain on this train and return to the confines of your own state. I am pleased to have been given these orders, and now that they are complete, I shall be on my way."

He clicked his heels and saluted once more, leaving Archibald to stand looking questioningly at the object in his hands.

Archibald opened the metal container, and there gleamed a silver medal. It was laid upon a mauve cushion, and Arnold's name was emblazoned on the front of it. Mr. Cunnings then glanced out of the railcar window to where more individuals, most likely from the end of the procession, were making their way across the platform. They looked just as ragged and beaten as Georgy. The only difference was that they were in cast-iron shackles that dragged across the ground and looked extremely heavy. No doubt in Archibald's mind that these too were prisoners.

Thinking first of leaving the train as to contact Arnold or at least any other member of *The Absolute Watch*—namely, Dr. Eicher or Pierre Libois—and realizing he would not receive a reply for a few days' time, he promptly turned around to sit back in his place in first-class and await the engine's rumble.

9

As Arnold's declaration was being read by the many denizens of the country, a buzz began to brew. Thousands of early risers were waking up to the words that he had so fervently displayed for them with the help of his subordinates. Opinions had begun to flurry, and with what seemed like passing moments, the general public was discussing the probable meaning of this doctrine.

"Ludicrous!" a man from the countryside exclaimed, who had fathered a family of numerous children. "How can you consciously neglect, not to mention exclude, a human being without seeming as though you do not possess a conscience at all?"

"I think it to be a sign of genius," his wife replied. "We must take care of our own flesh and blood at any cost. Not to do so would be an insult to our lineage." After this statement, she picked up her youngest child and cradled him in her arms.

Two university students were sipping caffeinated beverages in one of the local Downington cafés and were overheard by the other consumers as their debate became increasingly heated.

"How could one produce something so ignorant and selfish . . . ?" the younger of the two began seriously. "Is he not a human? Does he not have shortcomings and downfalls like the rest of us?"

"But every man is a political animal . . . ," his counterpart retorted with vibrato. "And this is rightly so. What makes us human is our consciousness of moral superiority. Without this recognition, we are but beasts. In that respect, those creatures have no concept of sin and are guiltless. So if he is a man, then he understands that others must be excluded for the benefit of a select group of people. If he is an animal, then he is inherently held unaccountable. Either way, your statement is invalid."

"So I suppose we should just ignore all of our wrongdoings?"

"Precisely. That is how we should proceed from our mistakes."

"Rubbish," the junior student lashed as he walked away from their sitting place, leaving the senior student to pay for their drinks.

Similar disagreements and affirmations were made all over Downington and spread at a hurried pace. Not only was Arnold's piece gaining attention, but it was also sparking physical representations of what he was attempting to accomplish. Throughout the week of its publication, numerous town halls in different counties of Downington were called to discuss the matter. Coalitions of like-minded individuals were formed out of the ensuing broken fragments. The mosaics that had formed began to appropriate competition between countrymen. Those in favor of Arnold thought it a splendid idea for him to run for a seat in government, concluding that his knowledge of societal circumstances made him a shoo-in candidate. Those who opposed Mr. Esche caught wind of this and deemed those who encouraged him unfit and mentally inept, for who could give a vote to an individual who lacked the capability of sympathy or empathy or understanding?

Signs began to appear on the front properties and in the windows of homes and apartments that read, "Us against Them" written in the official color of the state and "Hate Has No Home Here" that donned the phrase in numerous foreign languages. This division that began to arise among them left open spaces and voids in their thought processes and objective abilities. No longer was anything up for progressive debate. Private opinions and conclusions were held by citizens in relative secrecy unless it was previously seen or spoken openly that a pair or party agreed upon them bar none. When they found their way to speech or action, they became forceful and overbearingly affective.

For the past week, Genevieve was planning an offensive for the workers of *The Absolute Watch* so that they may fight against the unemployment forced upon them indefinitely. She began to hold small meetings in each department to rally proletariat support and suggested that they all choose a representative so they might be able to arrange higher-level talks with management. After a few brief suggestions and insistencies, no further progress had been made. It seemed that no matter what was discussed, they would all surely find themselves unable to sway any judgment. Genevieve herself became bothered by constant stalling. She was trying to help those who could not seemingly help themselves. Why was it that there was no agreement, whomever it would ultimately favor, that both sides could come to? Not a resolution whatsoever? She was spending all her time looking for an answer to these questions. Eventually, the workers of *The Absolute Watch* became downtrodden and depressed.

As Genevieve passed a few machinists in the cafeteria, she overheard them accepting their fate.

"There must surely be work elsewhere. There is a great demand for those who possess our skills with production capability."

His less-than-enthusiastic counterpart replied, "Yes, but we will we only meet the same fate elsewhere.

Pay has increased in the time we have dedicated to this establishment. We will once again be faced with base salary."

Genevieve was genuinely concerned for their well-being, but it was unfortunately apparent that Pierre Libois and his conspirators would have their way. Knowing these employees would be figuratively worked into the ground, Genevieve had an idea that sparked a flash of brilliance.

They were going to stop working, she realized. *So why don't they just stop working?*

At the end of one workday, feeling as though she now had the secret to retaining their positions, she gathered up the representatives from each department, as well as their constituents, to explain, "Tomorrow, just as everyone is arriving to start their shifts, none of us in our respective departments will go to work. Instead, we will all remain out front of *The Absolute Watch*'s doors and refuse entry to anyone attempting to continue its operation."

Few were interested in the prospect of not working in the morrow. Most of the employed were skeptical as to how this was to help any of them.

One packaging associate asked, "If we do not work, then how will we be paid?"

Others nodded in agreement.

"You will not be paid."

Nervous glances met her eyes.

"The idea is that the system of hierarchy will not benefit either! How could management be paid as well if no money is being made?"

Curious faces directed themselves to her attention.

"If we do not stand here tomorrow in solidarity, then we are nothing but a few splinters that they will meticulously pluck from their sides. Together we can change not only their method of operation but the minds that are strategically molded behind them. With this in our hearts, we cannot fail. If we force them down to our level, they will have no choice but to draw up a document that includes us all. Do I have your word that none will come tomorrow with the intent to continue their labor?"

Inspired by not only her words but her promises, they all agreed unanimously.

Feeling as though she had the support of her audience, she felt it prudent to leave them and find Pierre Libois to inform him that she and her group were not to be engaging in any suspicious activity and that their intent was pure. Perhaps he would even tear up his previous signature and start fresh with her on the spot.

Approaching the conference room, as she knew this was exactly where Mr. Libois was to be found, she felt confidence well up inside her chest cavity. She knocked thrice and was called in by none other than Pierre himself. As she pushed open the wooden door, she made her way up to the head of the conference table. Pierre was opening a letter while a plentitude of others were condensed into two piles, opened and unopened, beside him.

Without looking up, knowing exactly who had called upon him, he held firm his conviction, "I am sorry, Ms. Allman, but I will not void that contract under any circumstance."

The letter in his hands had been re-enveloped and put aside on top of the opened collection of letters.

Picking up another from the opposite pile and tearing it open with his hands, he went on, "Is there any other serious matter you have come to discuss?"

Not to be deterred, she cleared her throat to tell him to pay attention.

Becoming annoyed, Pierre obliged.

"I have just come to tell you that the whole of your department, as well as all others, will not be present for work in the morning. We have all come to an agreement that we will no longer labor for those who do not properly compensate us."

Pierre's expression did not change. "You have them in wholehearted support, I assume?"

"Definitely," she affirmed.

"I highly appreciate the forewarning. Is this all you have come to tell me?"

All she had to tell him . . . ? Could there be anything more detrimental to his future applications than this?

Genevieve was certain that Mr. Libois was not grasping what had just been revealed to him.

"I hope that you will be prepared for what is to come!" She announced this statement with great emphasis on the word *hope*. She turned on the spot and left the room.

Pierre hardly listened to Genevieve, although he grasped the meaning of her visit. He was much too preoccupied with the letters stacked before him on the conference table. These letters had been written to Arnold, in lieu of his absence brought to Mr. Libois by Sebastian, and concerned his article in the paper. There were equally as many praises as there were condemnations. As he waded through them, Pierre was becoming more and more confident in his decision to move forward with his ambitions. As there were two separate parties now forming at *The Absolute Watch*, the same had now been realized by the direction of the general public regarding the paper. When he finished reading a few more pieces of writing from the citizens of Downington, he thought it wise to visit the managers at *The Absolute Watch* at the end of the day to discuss the potential strike.

He made his way downstairs to the lobby, along with many other employees who were filing out of the front doors. A few seemed to be in high spirits; they were nudging each other in a playful manner and talking loudly. When they saw Pierre, they glanced in his direction but did not seem to notice him passing them. As he made his way to the main offices, the secretary too had gone home for the day. Remembering where they had last met, Mr. Libois showed himself down the back hall to the last room situated at the hallway's end. He knocked consistently on the door until someone had answered. The human resources manager opened the door to face Pierre. She was not surprised to see him, although it looked as if she was just about to leave the building herself.

"Hello, Mr. Libois," she began. "To what do I owe this late-afternoon pleasure?"

She led him into the room where they had previously discussed obtaining their upcoming incentives. He motioned for her to sit down, and guessing this would only take a moment or so, she obliged.

"I have some information concerning the contract that I have signed drawn up by management."

She eyed him suspiciously.

Pierre noticed this but continued, "Genevieve Allman came to the conference room to tell me that she will be leading the workers tomorrow morning in a picket to object their future."

She held up her hand and proclaimed, "I care not what the other employees do as it does not concern me. The document has been signed, and there is nothing that will change that."

"Oh, but there is," commented Pierre. "If there is a strong collection of individuals attempting to achieve this goal, then we will be the ones to pay dearly. Imagine if even one person is injured and files a claim against us. We could lose everything. The actions of all of these employees are unpredictable. The reputation of this paper could be ruined instantly, and then there would be nothing, monetarily speaking, for us to gain from it. I'm afraid it will only end in a negative outcome."

"Well, we cannot possibly stop them from amassing at their workplace. What would you propose that we do, Mr. Libois?"

Pierre had been thinking of a solution in the conference room and had already come to a brilliant conclusion.

"I propose that we do nothing to stop them from gathering. This way, it would look as though their protests were justified and that we are, in fact, the ones rightfully responsible for this indignation. We shall pretend to give in to their demands but only to gain the upper hand and procure enough funds to have them fired in the end. We will offer them a minuscule salary increase to make them think they have gained something for their troubles."

The human resources manager pondered the idea. She then spoke with an air of contemplative questioning, "But how could we afford this with our current increase? I don't believe that either the production and packaging or accounting head would be willing to give up their winnings to satisfy those who are to be eventually let go. I certainly will take nothing less than what has already been agreed upon."

Mr. Libois had already answered this question in his head and with resolution explained, "Ah, but that is where I have made a personal decision for myself. I will make an amendment to our document that removes my name as a benefactor of these allocated funds. This way, we can provide minute increases in the others' pay for a brief time until we are to do away with them."

She seemed to agree that this was plausible. "But how could you give up such a bonus? You must surely think that as a figurehead, you of all people would not sell yourself short."

"This is just a sacrifice that I am willing to make. The responsibility that one carries on one's shoulders can only be relieved of a burden by such an act. By removing myself from the seemingly questionable situation, I immediately have grounds to affect it."

Feeling satisfied by this proposal, the human resources manager agreed and thanked Pierre Libois for sharing such information with her. She promised to amend their document so that he would no longer gain any compensation from it. With this agreement, Pierre shook hands with the woman and bowed himself out.

The next morning, almost all the lower-ranking employees had shown up to stand outside of *The Absolute Watch*. Some had gone inside to work, not being able to neglect the fact that they had families to feed, while others took the opportunity to stay at home and take the day off since they would not be working anyway. Chatter naturally spread among those present, and there was an air of excitement beginning to bubble.

"I'm really glad we're gathered here under one pretense," a human resources assistant exclaimed. "These workers deserve an increase in pay. How can the paper not provide a decent salary for them?"

A staff accountant was looking less than thrilled and began to comment on the crowd's intentions, "We really should be inside getting to work. All this is doing is showing them that we are not dedicated to a higher cause. The whole community will think we are nothing but gadabouts."

Similar reactions and whispers flowed through the continual gathering of people on the business grounds. Genevieve was sharply dressed in proper business attire, holding a clipboard in front of her that listed points of interest in case they came across any opposition. No one present was sure what they were to be doing instead of standing and conversing with each other, but it seemed to them better than engaging in their usual labor. Pierre was looking out of the window in the conference room and moving his eyes about the scene below. He was confident that when he announced that the employees would be receiving raises, they would stand down at once and return to take up their posts inside *The Absolute Watch*. However, it was not yet time to reveal this to them, and he wanted to wait until the perfect moment to announce it.

The front grounds of *The Absolute Watch* were spilling over with bodies shuffling about. Genevieve was shocked that the number of attendees grew so large. Surely, all these people could not be employees. There was a man who was dressed much too fancily to ever be working on a machine, and there was a woman Genevieve spotted dressed in silk robes who was shaking hands with those she recognized to be employed in the packaging department.

Genevieve tried explaining the situation to herself, *This must be a result of Arnold's article. Word of mouth had probably gotten around to local residencies and establishments that there was a wage discrepancy here.*

After coming to this conclusion, she felt as though this had been the right course of action after all. For if there was support from the greater community, surely their demands could no longer be ignored and would be met with vigor.

Genevieve Allman was approached by the man and woman she had seen who did not belong to *The Absolute Watch*. She was met with glee as the workers had explained that she was the one who had brought this idea to fruition. They, and several other callers, praised her for her determination not to let this business run them out of personal decency.

Welling with appreciation and confidence, word began to gather that she was to give a speech.

One by one, people approached her and asked her to head for the front steps of *The Absolute Watch*. They told her to give word as to why they were all gathered and what course of action they were to take next. She began eagerly flipping through her notes to muster something better than prose, but when she arrived in front of the sea of what looked to her about a thousand people, she decided to speak impromptu.

"Thank you all very much for arriving here at the paper. It is my pleasure that so many of you have come out for this cause that we are all so passionate about."

There was a roar from the crowd, and even a few signs were starting to pop up into her view. One read, "Inclusion for All" and another, "Human: Here under Many Appropriate Notions."

This gave her a greater sense of purpose as she continued, "We have the power to spark change, and that is something no one can take away from us. This paper has provided income for those who otherwise might not be able to find work elsewhere. We must continue this tradition of equality for all."

As Genevieve heard similar yells of approval, she also began to hear ones of disapproval as well. As she investigated the crowd, peering into it with greater detail, she began to see images of a negative kind. One sign read,

"BAD BUSINESS = BAD OUTCOME," and another that was far from what she thought as appropriate, "FREEDOM OF PRESS, OR FREEDOM TO DIGRESS?"

As she began to continue what little she had left to say, Genevieve stopped almost instantly as the crowd began to sway back and forth. It was now extremely loud among those present in the mass of individuals. Tension was clearly rising. Objects were being tossed carelessly in the air. Unexpectedly, the window from the conference room had burst open with a clattering bang; a large bell had been attached to the window from the inside. Pierre was hanging out of the window, and everyone looked up at him, following the unsuspecting noise it had made.

"My dear workers!" he bellowed. "I have decided to give raise to your salary in place of my own. Please do come inside. A free lunch is being provided as well!"

With this statement, everything seemed to be quelled. Those who were indeed employed at *The Absolute Watch* dropped whatever quarrel they had with its management and swept inside at this announcement. Those who were merely present for show of support dropped their banners and headed away from the foreground, sensing the protest was over.

Genevieve could hear the workers calling out in relief, "And I thought I was to be fired! Happy day!"

Another was pushing his way through the hustle and bustle, panting, "I am quite hungry, let me through!"

A packaging associate was conversing among his friends, "He's going to take a cut of pay for us? He must genuinely understand our needs!"

Genevieve, too, was pleased with the outcome. However, she did not believe it was as genuine of an act as the crowd believed it to be. She was rightfully skeptical of Pierre. Why had he shown such a gesture of good faith at a time when he was going to strip anyone and everyone of their current possessions? After the entrance area of *The Absolute Watch* cleared, as many shuffled their way into the dining area, Genevieve made her way upstairs to the conference room to confront Mr. Libois.

When she knocked on the conference room door, as it was already ajar it swung open of its own accord. Pierre Libois was staring out of the now-closed window where he had just made his announcement minutes before. He had his hands neatly arranged behind his back and saw Genevieve's reflection in the windowpane.

As she approached, thinking of what she was going to say to him, he promptly turned around and spoke first, "You have achieved what you wished, have you not?"

Although she agreed with him, she asked indignantly, "The real question is, why have you given in so easily? You cannot have possibly done this with good intention."

"And why is that?" he asked reproachfully.

"Because I know all too well that you want to be in control of this establishment, which means you will do whatever it takes to achieve that goal. You may be able to fool the others, but you cannot fool me! You do not care about those people any more than you care about the things that Arnold is writing."

"You are correct," he breathed heavily.

Stunned but continuing to let him speak, Genevieve waited for him to start up again.

"I do not care for these workers at all. They are simply a source of labor for me to achieve my ends. I do not believe myself to be wrong in this, however you seem to judge me as if it is a crime. These people are not of the same fabric as we are. They do not possess motivation or any self-will at all. They are not even sure of what they desire, let alone what they need. They simply move on with the ebb and flow. They wish to be taken care of. I wish that I, too, was able to throw such cautions to the wind, for lack of a better description, but I just cannot. I am able to rule, and so rule I must, even though it is at the expense of others.

"Not everyone can be satisfied in such a manner. I myself have just given up my salary to prove this. Do you hear me clearly? Not everyone can be satisfied! It is just a measure of existence. No matter what is at stake and who is involved, the variation will always be 51 to 49 percent. 'Equality' and 'equilibrium' are mere fancies we like to assign to ourselves so that we may attempt to balance out this difference to the closest decimal point or fraction. If you cannot agree with me on this, then I am afraid to tell you that you just have no understanding of existential simplicity."

Wishing that she had not even gone to see him at all, she realized that there was no arguing with him. This man was so set in believing he was above others that he could not possibly move down to their level and gain their perspective.

"These individuals are not as useless as you claim them to be. They have feelings and aspirations that you could never dream of!"

"Yes, but dreaming and doing are two completely different scopes of reality, and believe me, they are quite useful to me. If you could see this, then perhaps you would join me instead of standing up for those who choose ignorance over concrete evidence."

Once again, unable to convince him that he was indeed the ignorant one, Genevieve slipped out of the conference room, leaving the wooden door remaining half open.

Before Pierre had a moment to focus his own thoughts, there was a knock on the closed portion of the door, and half of Sebastian's frame became visible between it and the wall. Making eye contact with him, Pierre motioned him to push the door further open.

"Another letter to Dr. Eicher from Arnold," he announced.

Handing him the envelope, Sebastian bowed himself out of the room, not bothering to ask what the letter entailed. Pierre went and sat down at a random chair on the side of the conference table and read silently:

Dr. Eicher,

How splendid my travels have been! I have learned so much about the world around us, and I am keen to hear what people are saying about my article. I hope it will have had the effect I was looking to produce, although you may not approve of such baiting. Nonetheless, when I return before the end of this year, I will be electing a successor based on all collective research. I hope that the three of you have some interesting points to make. Please tell Genevieve that I demand her to be at the final presentations. I do not want her to miss out on valuable information.

Best regards,

Arnold Esche

10

After his latest trip to Joanne Freeman's estate, Dr. Eicher was sleeping for unusually long hours unperturbed. He would turn in around midevening and would sleep well into the next afternoon. In the short span of time that he was awake during the day, he began penning a few questionnaires for the young tutor to answer in an attempt to put together a dossier for Arnold.

After beginning with various points of light conversation, Dr. Eicher thought it best to delve deeper into inquiries of personal events so that he might truly reveal Henry's mental state. Their last encounter had been one of great concern to the doctor because the youth had been overflowing with bother. Why had he not made formal contact? Was he dealing with personal affliction?

He certainly was having a kind of fit, the doctor admitted.

Toward the end of the week, Erich Eicher had called upon Francis Thompson to ask him to make the trip into the countryside to fetch Henry, hoping that he would be present at Joanne Freeman's. Mr. Thompson accepted this with ardor, hoping that, in turn, he would once again be able to speak with the latter's driver, Edward Montclair.

As the doctor sat patiently awaiting the youth's potential arrival, he began hopefully daydreaming about Joanne Freeman. The doctor was soon to be making his way to her abode for a dinner party, and he was keen to the idea that this was where they would finally cement a relationship that had been, in his eyes, moving steadfastly into formation. He imagined the lovingly intoxicated pair taking long walks about the grounds of his home, their hands clasped together and the sun shining brightly upon them.

Transfixed as he had become, the doctor awoke from his thoughts just as the front door to his foyer had creaked open. Francis Thompson and Henry could be heard conversing in the foyer, and announcing that he would be taking his leave, Mr. Thompson promptly closed the door behind him and made his exit.

Henry waltzed into the tearoom, dressed overwhelmingly flamboyant for a young man, where Dr. Eicher was seated at his desk. Standing up to formally greet him, the doctor, hand outstretched, made his way over to Henry, and the two shook warmly.

"Thank you for making this journey at my request," the doctor started. "I am pleased to see that you happened to be present at Ms. Freeman's this afternoon."

"Very much so," the youth answered, "as I take up my residence there."

The doctor nodded in place of this new piece of information. "Please sit down."

In the corner of the tearoom, there was a small table with two chairs at either end. Both gentlemen sat down and made eye contact. Dr. Eicher led the conversation.

"If I may," the doctor began, "why is it that someone of no relation resides in the house of a countess?"

Attempting to remain nonchalant, Dr. Eicher was asking this question more for himself rather than keeping an open window of communication, but he knew it went along with his previous plan nonetheless.

"I am there strictly for her relation, as a matter of fact. Peter and I are dear friends, and my lessons come at no cost. He is a delicate individual and needs constant attention. If it were not for him, I daresay, I would be thrown from the house immediately."

The doctor noted this and began to press on, "And why would you be banished in such a matter?"

"Joanne Freeman absolutely despises me."

The doctor was now fully invested in his words. "Surely, this cannot be true?"

"But it is, sir," Henry admitted. "I am assigned to tutor Peter under the condition of our friendship. I have great talent for such teaching, however he will not listen to anyone else. I often encourage him to abandon his studies, this is under my personal pretense that someone of his incapability and less than willingness has utterly no use for them. I try and coerce Joanne into freeing him from long hours and constant, immovable obstacles, and that is why she hates me so. He should be engaging in play and creativity instead of being pushed into learning things he does not understand."

The doctor sat pondering the youth's statements. Ignoring the supposition that Joanne could produce such spite, Dr. Eicher asked him, "How did it come to pass then that you, someone of a higher intelligence, and Peter, someone of a lower intelligence, so to speak, came to be so close?"

"The first thing you must realize is that the extremely intelligent and the extremely unintelligent possess unmistakable similarities."

Henry thought back in his memory for a moment or two and then began.

"We met during our elementary years. At this level of education, as children are intermingled for a time being until it is clear which path they should take in academics, we spent hours and hours engaging in conversation about nothing at all. That was the true beauty of the whole situation. We had a few interests in common, and these were strong enough for us to hold a tight bond.

"As I was recruited by school officials in our middle years to participate in more engaging and difficult sets of problems, Peter was chosen to remain behind and learn at a much slower pace. This did not stall our interactions, and the establishment did not hinder our friendship. Eventually, Peter stopped going to school of his own accord, and I, moving ever so expediently into theories and applications, decided to discontinue my studies to help him navigate the rest of his basic disciplines.

"As I finally got him to keep at his schoolwork, he barely achieved completion. Wonderful, I thought. Now we could put an end to all this hubbub, and he could begin to live a life of freedom for himself. However, Joanne saw this as just another stepping-stone on the way to improving his image and senses. She enrolled him in university, and as expected, he failed every course. Reluctantly she asked me to return to his side and help him, ready as I was, through this new set of trials and tribulations. This is where we are today. I feel extremely woeful for him. If he could break away from Ms. Freeman, he'd be able to succeed in a way that obliges his limited talents."

"But why then does he stay in his current predicament? Surely, Ms. Freeman does not have complete control over him?"

"As I have explained previously, he is of a fragile nature. He needs to be taken care of. If I were not around to help him, she would be figuratively destroying his life. Taking any chance, she could make sure he lived exactly the life she wanted for him. I am afraid that I, too, am growing incessantly tired of the fact. I myself am finding it difficult to continue facades of her definition of progression."

Dr. Eicher was listening intently.

"I would like to apologize for my outburst the last time we met. I had been thinking about that chain of events for some time, and I suppose I felt the need to make someone listen."

The doctor accepted the apology gracefully.

"Joanne had explained to me that you were a doctor, and I decided that you would be a perfect candidate for my speculations under the pretense of professionalism. I hope that I was correct in this assumption."

"You were, my dear boy," Dr. Eicher assured Henry, attempting to make the youth feel comfortable and tell him more. "You can share with me anything you'd like. You can confide in me your worries without hesitation."

Henry looked down at the table, gathering his troubles. Drawing a large breath of oxygen, he continued, "Although I am greatly fond of Peter and want to help him to the best of my abilities, I am afraid that I am growing ever far apart from his situation and selfishly focusing on my own."

Thinking this was the climax of Henry's evolution of speech, the doctor remained still and focused earnestly.

"After much thought and conviction, I have decided that I would like very much to perish. Nothing in this life seems fulfilling enough to continue what I have experienced as a most overly drudging, extended beating of a heart. To those I will have to leave behind, namely Peter, I am unequivocally distraught. However, we all must face the end alone. I have visited the plausibility of taking my own life, however I do not believe that would be a fitting exit in the objective sense. I want those close to me, as well as those who believe their knowledge of ethics to be the law of the land, to wholeheartedly understand why they are to accept and embrace my departure rather than leave it to me to pack my own bags and run before they have a chance to question my motivations. Death with dignity would be the best course of action in my eyes. I would like to be administered medical euthanasia, to be put into a permanently deep sleep. Can one lobby their own death? I believe it to be achievable. As a matter of fact," Henry said, pronouncing his words with deep calm and composure, something that surprised the doctor greatly, "I have written a proclamation of this to our Board of Governors of The Commerce and Wealth of England just this week and have already received a reply that they will be willing to listen to me plead my case."

He eyed the doctor intently, hoping for a reply. When he did not receive one, he asked, "Will you testify at this hearing on my behalf?"

Stunned for a moment or two at the prospect of himself, as well as publicly elected officials, helping this troubled individual end his own life, Dr. Eicher began to formulate that this would be the ultimate presentation for Arnold Esche. As the youth's eyes began to widen, the doctor, pushing moral intrusions aside, agreed.

Henry held out a hand, and Dr. Eicher took it only for a quick moment. A brief silence fell over the two until Henry restarted their conversation.

"So, Doctor, I take it that you are quite adept in the field of human understanding. Please, explain to me the notion of paid labor. I understand the objective sense in having a job and making money, but why is it that some individuals tediously work their lives away?"

This is a fair question, thought the doctor, for although this youth did not want to continue into the realm of a self-sustaining future, he understood his curiosities.

"We as individuals have needs that we must fulfill to continue our wants. We need food, water, and shelter so that we may pursue these wants. These immediate needs supersede these wants until there is nothing left but complete satisfaction and fulfillment. Unfortunately, many workers do not succeed in this although they have sustained life long enough to achieve a piece of this want.

Some are simply satisfied, as in your case, it seems, to want nothing more than need. Here, one only partakes in the bare minimum. You do not see the need in working because you will not have sustained life for an extensive period. Therefore, work does seem to be a subjective nuance in one way or another."

"I see," continued Henry. "And what do you do for work, Doctor? I assume you run a practice out of this house?"

"On the contrary," he said, speaking as though he did not wish this to be so, "I work for a newspaper. However, I have taken some time to myself explore other options." He concluded his speech with a lie because he was using this young man to achieve his ends.

"That sounds like more of a misfortune than employment to me."

The doctor was nonplussed at the youth's reproachful utterance.

"I have read many newspapers, and they are all nothing but gossip and lies."

"That is false. Many great writings and pieces of interest have come from print."

The youth was not convinced. "I had read a curt article recently that made me question the author's integrity. It was stupidly written and gave an air of pretentiousness I could not ignore. That Mr. Esche must be a truly loathsome man."

As he heard the name of Mr. Esche escape Henry's breath, his complexion went pale white.

"Sir . . . Doctor? Are you all right?"

Dr. Eicher's head began to flood with the realization of what was happening all around him. Arnold. Archibald. Pierre. *The Absolute Watch.*

Hastily trying to gather himself, the doctor asked the youth, "When was this article published?"

"A few days ago. I take it there has been some backlash and, quite surprisingly, support for this man."

Without seeming as though he was throwing the boy out, he quickly called Francis Thompson back from his residence and thanked the youth for his time, promising once again he would be there to support him at the time of his scheduled meeting with the Board of Governors of The Commerce of Wealth of England. When he was finally alone, his mind began to rage at the fact that he had been so ignorant as to not pay attention to what was happening at *The Absolute Watch.*

Arnold was definitely disappointed at my absence although he granted it to me. Dr. Eicher's head hung low. *I have lost the position for myself.*

Thinking for a moment of giving up on his prospective promotion, and as tired as he was, he ultimately decided to go and seek out Arnold at *The Absolute Watch.*

After Francis Thompson returned from Joanne's for a second time, faster than he normally would have traveled at the doctor's request, Dr. Eicher pleaded with him to make one more journey on his behalf. Obliging, Mr. Thompson led the doctor down the stone path of his property and into the horse and buggy. The gloomy weather had not yet begun to blacken into nightfall, although it was fast approaching. As they started their trek into the city, the doctor was hard-pressed to find a reason not to berate himself.

Surely, Archibald has already returned from his journey, treasure trove in hand, and Pierre probably has pages of information while I have nothing to show for my lousy effort!

As they rolled into the tight-knit residential area lining the city center, Dr. Eicher stared blankly at the homes of strangers. A few panes of glass were glowing with candlelight, hoping to fend off the impending darkness. He appreciated the lack of space between these individual buildings and realized that it must be quite difficult to share so much with those with whom they most likely had some form of forced contact. He began to spot uniformity of structure and color—and of a few of them, they stood in a row like a barrier blocking a taller entrance. As he continued to gaze interestingly as they swept past his vision, he noticed signs that hung in these windows, some of which were planted into the foreground of the front walkways.

At a particularly shabby-looking, paint-peeling eyesore, there was a myriad of large slogans in blazing red letters that included "Our Country First" and "Build Up Fortifications."

Quite isolationist, thought the doctor. *How could someone living among so many others be capable of such tendencies?*

As they moved hurriedly along, and into the heart of the city, a large Victorian-style house of stone, complete with foliage and flowers, had one sign in blue that read, "Hate Has No Home Here."

Placed directly under this proclamation were a few phrases written in many foreign languages the doctor knew to be of distant origins.

Strange, remarked the doctor to himself. *Why have a foreign tongue upon a sign when hardly anyone within the confines of this city could decipher it?*

More and more sightings of this kind met the doctor's vision as he pulled up slowly to the front gates of *The Absolute Watch.* It was now evening, and a few employees were still making their way out of *The Absolute Watch's* front door after their shifts had ended.

Dr. Eicher thanked Mr. Thompson for his services and asked if he could please spare him a bit more time while he went to check in on the day's events. Nodding in agreement, Dr. Eicher removed himself from his seat and made his way through to the front doors. The entrance hall was now empty. Although he had only been gone for about two weeks' time, the halls seemed to echo strangely as if great chatter had been gone only but a moment before he arrived. It was not foreign to him, although he felt an eerie feeling airing upon his senses.

First, he decided, he would go up to Arnold's office to get a direct source of information that would not be at all watered down. As he climbed the staircase and made his way to the top of the structure, twisting and turning down the halls, he noticed before he had reached its door that Arnold's dwelling was empty. No light was emitting from it, and as he went to test the handle, it was locked.

Searching in his mind for a second option, he concluded the next best place to look for someone of rank was the conference room. Feeling that at least one person would be there at some extra piece of work, he made his way back down the hall and around another corner. Light was indeed emitting from the crack beneath this door, and unlike Arnold's entrance, he promptly rapped upon it three times.

"Come in," came a familiar voice that the doctor had not heard for some time.

As he stepped inside the room, Pierre Libois was sitting at the table's head, a stack of letters lying on either side of him. Thinking this was Genevieve meddling in his affairs, he did not pick up his head.

The doctor was not so keen upon this lack of greeting and spoke, "Good evening, Mr. Libois."

At the sound of the doctor's voice, Pierre immediately jerked his head upward and realized Erich Eicher was just beyond the doorway, looking down at him from a position of poise.

"Doctor," he exclaimed, "you have been gone for quite some time. How are you feeling?"

Pierre had obviously thought me sick, the doctor determined agreeably.

"I am fine, Pierre. I hope you have not been working too hard?"

"Hard work is for those who are not in such a position as we are."

They both gave shallow scoffs.

"And what have I missed in my absence?" asked the doctor, trying not to sound as desperate as he really felt at the lack of current news he possessed.

Pierre, knowing the doctor was not aware of his doings, thought it best not to keep any more secrets and pulled the edition of the paper with Arnold's writing on the front page out from a stack of the current week's prints on a chair adjacent to him.

"This, though I'm sure you have already read it." He held out the paper for Dr. Eicher to take.

As he walked over to Pierre and took the paper from his hands, he read Arnold's article in full. Frowning at all that was written and feeling stupid because this was, indeed, the first time he had seen it, he allowed his expression to harden.

"No. I have not yet seen this atrocity, and I am ashamed that it has been published. Who allowed this sort of temperament to make front page representing our lauded company?" He was now beginning to understand the frivolous signs that he passed on his trip to *The Absolute Watch.*

Pierre had expected this sort of reaction out of the doctor whether he viewed the article previously or not.

"Arnold had asked for it to be published, there was nothing any of us could do to prevent it."

Almost expecting this answer, the doctor explained, "Of course he would have asked for it to be published! This is his business, is it not? He expects complete control simply because he foots the bill for everything. However, this does not make his opinion truth. Do you not see the damage this may cause? If anyone else but I understood the delicate differences between ethos, pathos, and logos, this would have been shot down at once. Who is responsible for bringing this to the editing room and having it published?"

At first, Pierre Libois thought of revealing to Dr. Eicher that it was, indeed, him that asked for the article's publication. He could not possibly fire him for doing so. Although, Pierre pondered, if someone else were to take blame for this incident, then he would be free to keep his previous plans in place, refraining him from tarnishing his image in a way that could affect Arnold's choice for the successor of *The Absolute Watch*.

Thinking that over, looking as though he were trying to remember the real culprit of the matter, Pierre spoke, "It was a boy by the name of Sebastian. He is one of Arnold's staff clerks. I had overheard it from one of the managers earlier this week. I believe a move has already been made against him, regarding his firing, as he made to publish it without proper approval."

Taking this as a satisfactory answer, Dr. Eicher nodded in approval. "Very well then," he affirmed. "As for your project, I assume all is going well?"

Unaware that the doctor was not only avoiding but also helping in his plot to become the sole owner of *The Absolute Watch*, Pierre confided to the doctor, "I am very proud of my progress, that is for sure. I only hope that it reveals the true nature of people in their natural habitat. This way, we will all have a better understanding of the future events to come."

Nervously comparing the two of them in this feat, the doctor responded, "I see. Well, it should be in no time now that Arnold will decide upon a victor. I hope that this task will end on positive terms."

"I as well," agreed Mr. Libois.

"I will return tomorrow to speak with Arnold about cleaning up this mess that has been spilled over Downington so that we may continue to repolish our prestigious name."

"Until then," spoke Pierre.

The doctor bowed out of the conference room and made his way back to the carriage where Francis Thompson was awaiting his return.

Pierre spent the rest of the evening at *The Absolute Watch* reading more and more letters the general public had sent in regarding Arnold's article. Did Dr. Eicher honestly not see them nor inquire about them? Looking over one letter about wanting to burn *The Absolute Watch* to the ground, he stopped to think on what Dr. Eicher had said to him about the former's abilities. Could the doctor truly recognize the differences between ethical thought so clearly as to reveal Pierre's true intentions? Clearly, he knew that something was wrong regarding the article; however, to what extent had Pierre led him to believe this?

Realizing his former encounters with the doctor, Mr. Libois concluded that the latter did have a special talent in dissecting probability regarding the outcome of events. In understanding this, Pierre would eventually have to answer for all the behind-the-scenes activities that went on while the doctor, Archibald, and Arnold were absent. He was determined, however, to make sure that he was the one to come out on top.

I must keep this charade afloat, he decided.

First, he would have to convince Sebastian to take the fall for him, promising him a reward in return. Second, he would have to make sure Arnold was to be on his side of the publishing—easily achievable for he was the one who wrote it and he surpassed them all in rank. Arnold would have to get over the fact that Pierre took the place of Dr. Eicher. Satisfied with these paths of achievement, Pierre continued to read the letters sent to *The Absolute Watch*.

He was thinking, *A concerted effort will beat an individual one nine times out of ten, and I will make bet on those odds anytime until the end of time.*

11

The very next morning would be the first occurrence wherein important members of *The Absolute Watch* were to gather and discuss current events that had recently taken place. This was the best opportunity for them to converse. Quarrels had just been settled among management, and things were beginning to smooth out on all platforms. Arnold's article produced ripples in the community and the workplace, but now the general public had moved on in their daily lives; and although traces of its publication were still relevant, it was talked about less and less as the days gradually marched forward.

The menace that was Arnold's writing had shifted to the anatomical figure of the man who wrote them once he stepped through the threshold of his business. He was hardly noticed as he waltzed into the entrance hall; however, he was not in a mood to hang about anywhere but his reserved area of comfort. Making his way up the staircase and down the same hall he had traveled hundreds of times before, he unlocked his wooden door and noticed how empty his quarters felt. He had not been in a fortnight.

Deciding he would at least try to interact with at least one person to affirm that everything was in order, he made his way to the conference room. Hoping to find Genevieve or Dr. Eicher, the man he put in charge of operations, he walked into the conference room with anticipation only to find Pierre Libois sitting at the table's head, reading the last bit of letters that had been received by *The Absolute Watch* regarding Arnold's article.

"Mr. Libois, I did not expect to find you here so early. How are you?"

Pierre got up from his seat startled but shook Arnold's hand in ardor. "I am well, Arnold, very well."

Pierre hoped that Arnold had not spoken to anyone else yet and asked him if he had done so in the form of an inquiry.

"No, I have just arrived here by myself. Would you happen to know where I can find Dr. Eicher?"

Pierre teetered on his reply for a moment, and then, realizing now was the opportunity to be completely truthful, he revealed everything to Arnold. First, he noted the doctor's extended absence, explaining Erich Eicher would be arriving today to speak later in the afternoon. Mr. Libois continued to explain that it was he who had been receiving and opening the letters addressed to Dr. Eicher and that it was he who had published the article that Arnold had penned. He spoke with Arnold about the backlash of the writing and that it was he himself, Pierre, that had been reading letters for the past few days on the subject submitted by residents of the city. He even told Arnold about the futile protest at *The Absolute Watch* and how he had relinquished his pay so that he could provide the workers with extra salary so they would return to work.

Upon hearing this lament, Arnold was taken aback. He did not anticipate this flow of admittance that was thrown upon him.

However, he pondered for a moment then inquired, "So the article was published then, correct? People threw a fuss, did they not?"

Pierre nodded his head in confirmation.

"Well, that settles it then!" breathed Arnold, relieved. "That is all that I had hoped for. Thank you for taking up my request, even though it did not go according to how I planned it."

As Arnold finished those words, Genevieve Allman opened the door to the conference room, hands balled in fists at her sides.

"You!" she exclaimed.

"I," Mr. Esche replied gleefully. "How are you, Genevieve? It is so good to see you."

"I cannot say the same," Genevieve said tersely. "You need to speak with the workers here immediately and apologize to them for your insolence. I have been trying very hard at mending the relationship between them and those like him," pointing to Pierre, "who sit around doing nothing all day—expecting positive result after result. Your words have been very harsh, and they have done nothing but further the divide in a gap that has been growing rapidly ever since you took to the front page. You have tarnished this paper's reputation and insulted its readers." With this last sentence, Genevieve put all the pent-up feelings she had into it.

"Insult them?" Arnold began. "And how is that possible when they are the ones to read it? I cannot force someone to be involved in anything, let alone use their eyes for them! Pierre here has just informed me of the last few days' events, and I can assure you that you are the one leading them in false pretense. They are very much helpless, and you are doing nothing for them unless you call instilling false hope a service."

"Why then did you instruct me to take on the operations of the paper?" A valid question.

"I gave you that opportunity to keep you busy. I did not want you to get the idea in your head that you had any control over the employees. Sure, you may direct them in a sense of physicality, but never would I allow you to make decisions for them! I am humbled that I have individuals like Mr. Libois that understand the difference between objective labor and subjective direction. There is a delicate balance between them that I am sure you do not understand."

"How do I not understand this? What is it that I do not possess that makes me unworthy of procuring this business?"

"Simplicity!" Arnold broke out in a voice of exasperation. "You do not realize that some people just do better than others. They are not better, in a sense of purpose or societal hierarchy, but they do better! Better effort and better planning produce stronger willpower that not all possess. This is the true divide, and it cannot be ignored."

"But that is not equality! There is a solution where all can be equal."

Finished with this conversation, Arnold, who said nothing more, held up a hand to Genevieve. Arnold now addressed both her and Pierre.

"We will be able to speak on the matter later when Dr. Eicher arrives. When he does, Mr. Libois, the pair of you will be able to present your findings to me, and I will select a victor to be in sole possession of *The Absolute Watch*."

Pierre's eyes suddenly glowed at this statement. Genevieve turned on the spot and left the room in a state of great animosity.

Arnold turned to Mr. Libois and proclaimed, "Now I will take a period of rest. Please call to me when the doctor arrives, and we can continue on with this business."

He shook Pierre's hand once more and left the conference room, shutting the door as he let himself out. Feeling pleased with himself, Pierre sat back down at the table and opened the last letter that had been received by the general public.

It read:

> We are now in tatters. All of us. Who will survive here? A question no one can answer.

As he awoke in the afternoon, Dr. Erich Eicher lay awake in his bed feeling dizzier and drowsier than ever. He attempted to shut his eyes once more, hoping to sleep longer; however, his body seemed to be too immobile to shut his eyes again. He tried to think on the past day's events, but fuzz and small popping noises entered his thoughts as though he had been drinking heavily. He decided to muster up all his strength, difficult as this was, and sit up straight. To his surprise, all the inhabitant obstacles had been cleared, and he was able to open and shut his eyes once again.

Removing himself from the comfort of his resting place, he got dressed and made his way downstairs to the tearoom. Combining his thoughts of the two meetings he had yesterday with Henry and Pierre, he quickly moved to his desk area and began preparing parchment and quill as to continue his dossier for Arnold. He wrote that Henry was to be meeting with the Board of Governors of The Commerce and Wealth of England to discuss the possibility of removing the life from his person. The doctor created a footnote here that read, "Terminally Ill."

As he completed a brand-new set of questions for Henry, he worked diligently for the next hour attempting to dissect the youth even further. Deciding that he was finished, he rolled up the parchment and tied it with a piece of string. As he tied its knot, he glanced at a letter on the corner of his desk that was tied in the same material. He stared at it for a few moments, not recognizing what it was or from whom the letter was. Piecing together his work for Arnold before him, along with the prospect of obtaining *The Absolute Watch*, he suddenly remembered who handed him the forgotten letter. Just before his departure east, Archibald Cunnings had given him this note to deliver to the Board of Governors of The Commerce and Wealth of England in his absence.

But surely, he would've returned by now, surmised the doctor.

Nevertheless, he pocketed Mr. Cunnings's letter, anticipating that he would return it to him when he eventually arrived back at work. A few moments later, having already called upon Francis Thompson to take them around the city and back to *The Absolute Watch* for the second time in two days, a knock had been placed at the front door. Taking long strides toward the source of the sound, Dr. Eicher opened it, and there stood a figure of whom he was previously familiar.

Edward Montclair smiled as they met face-to-face.

"I have a letter from Ms. Joanne Freeman."

The doctor, expecting this warmly, motioned him to proceed.

Mr. Montclair read aloud:

> Dear Erich,
>
> I have written to Father in regard to my loathing for the family business, and to my great surprise, he has agreed to talk matters over with me before his party! I am in jubilation that my voice is finally being heard. This, along with the prospect that I will be able to spend some more time alone with you, has thrown me into a great state of dazzling prospect and longing for the future. I hope that you are well and are thinking earnestly about me. I shall see you very soon.
>
> With my sincerest feelings,
>
> Joanne Freeman

At the signature, Mr. Montclair looked slyly at the doctor, whose heart simply dropped.

Finally, regaining his composure, Dr. Eicher thanked the former and shook his hand graciously.

Instead of bowing himself out of the doorframe, Mr. Montclair asked the doctor eagerly, "Excuse me, sir, but is Francis here perchance?"

"He should be here any moment," the doctor replied.

Just then, the man in question pulled up at the front of the stone path in his conveyance. Noticing this, Edward Montclair turned and made his way down to the carriage and spoke a few words with him. After a brief exchange of words, he returned to his own method of transport and was off. When he reached the doctor still standing on the threshold with the door wide open, Francis Thompson looked positively smitten.

"What has he spoken with you about?" asked the doctor imploringly.

"He has asked me to accompany him to Joanne's father's party!" Francis replied excitedly.

The morning after Arnold's return, Genevieve Allman had much less to do than usual at *The Absolute Watch*. She arrived late to his combination bedroom and office to pick up her secretarial duties, only to find out that her boss had not yet risen.

First morning upon his return, and it seems that he is still somewhere else.

She imagined him under the covers snoring loudly. Seeing as she could not yet perform her limited duties she, decided to walk around the levels of the paper and observe its population.

She passed the writing and editing room where tens of employees were scrawling notes upon long pieces of parchment, attempting to amass them into a worthy story. Next, she went down to the production floor to see how they were carrying along since they had been given monetary incentives. Nothing seemed to have changed as a few members were taking unscheduled naps in the corners behind where their machines stood. Others, who were indeed awake, were mindlessly pressing buttons and staring into space while strapping bundles of finished products together, seemingly in a dream much like their counterparts. Genevieve understood this was not the most enthralling task, but she wondered whether or not they put purpose into what they were doing.

Low pay will do that to a person, she concluded.

As she attempted to walk back the way she came, her path was blocked by the packaging and production manager who walked straight past all the snoozing operators without the bat of an eye. Genevieve greeted her, but the woman seemed to be slightly preoccupied.

"I am resigning," she admitted to Ms. Allman.

"But why?" Genevieve started. "Surely, you are being paid enough?"

She turned and left Genevieve standing in the middle of the production floor.

"A bad feeling about this business,"she had said. Impossible, thought Ms. Allman. *The reputation of this place alone was in good standing, whether or not Arnold had published that piece of rubbish.*

She made her way back upstairs, thinking that Arnold might finally be awake, and alas, the light was on in his room. She strode over to it, knocked, and stood back as the door swung open.

Mr. Esche smiled as he saw that his young secretary was standing at his residence awaiting his instruction.

"Good morning," he bellowed.

Genevieve merely spluttered, "Do you have my notes for the day?"

"Ah yes," Arnold turned and made his way to his desk. He handed Genevieve one piece of paper that read:

Meeting in the conference room at 17:00.

Feeling as though this were his idea of a joke, she said no more and made her way to the conference room to prepare.

As she made her way into the said room, Pierre was again the sole individual sitting there at its table. He was not reading letters but writing something down, probably for Arnold and the rest to hear. He picked up his head to see Genevieve, and he too gave her a smirk. She ignored him and began rummaging in a box of quills and ink to

"That is not at all the problem, my dear. It is just th: I have talked with the accounting and human resourc managers, and it seems that they will not be hiring anoth manager to take over production duties. If I remain here will be doing twice the work for no more incentive."

She does look quite tired, thought Ms. Allman.

"I came to seek you out to ask you if you would n quit this place as well and join me somewhere else as assistant?"

Genevieve was shocked to hear this. *But*, she thoug momentarily, *an assistant?*

Surely, she was in that position already, and she doing much more than that for Arnold now.

"I would enjoy your confidence and prowess very m wherever I should go. I just have a bad feeling about business in the long term. With my résumé as a mana I should have no trouble being put on elsewhere. Wha you say?"

Genevieve thought hard for a length of seconds, ultimately, she decided that *The Absolute Watch* needed with Arnold and his cronies around.

"I am sorry, but I will have to decline. This p needs me."

Understanding her decision, the packaging production manager shook her hand firmly and sai wish you all the best. Please do not hesitate to seek m in the future."

set upon the table for the conference to come. She fetched receptacles for water and placed them on the table, making space for four of them. Pierre looked as though he were attempting to engage Ms. Allman in conversation; however, she kept her eyes firmly on the table.

He cleared his throat anyway and began, "I hope that you will sit in on this discussion with all of us, you should be making a place for yourself as well."

Rolling her eyes when she was not facing him, she replied, "There is no point, seeing as how I am not to be included in the conversation."

"But does that not mean you can still hear what is being discussed?"

This was certainly true. She had, after all, been indirectly included in *The Absolute Watch*'s raffling, and she was never ignorant to its ultimate changing of hands.

"I will only be present because I am Arnold's secretary. It is a matter of business, and I will only treat it as such."

"I would not have it any other way of course!" Pierre was obviously excited. "You know," he began, "if I am to be the one to take reins of the paper, I would very much like for you to be a part of it. I imagine that you could do a great deal under my counsel."

"I do not think so," she broke into the open air.

"And why not? I know you very well. Together we could do this business much good. I would even consider putting you in a management position."

"I would only do such a thing if it were on my own terms. Nothing less."

"And what are your terms?" He seemed very interested in this statement.

"To do things on my own. To have no decisions made for me. I am quite capable of sailing my own ship."

Pierre became silent but mouthed under his breath, "Alone we are but objects. Ones to be controlled at that."

As five o'clock came round, Arnold waited in the conference room half an hour early. Currently, all employees of *The Absolute Watch* were getting ready to leave for the day. Mr. Esche began thinking about his recent journey abroad and came to the personal conclusion that it was the best thing he'd done in quite a while, perhaps just as great as starting this paper.

Genevieve arrived a moment or so later to receive Arnold's confirmation that everything was set up properly. She waited with him standing in the corner. Next, Pierre had returned, for he was in the conference room almost all day and merely left so Arnold could be the first one formally there. He sat opposite Mr. Esche at the head of the table on the other end. Pierre took out his notes and began to read them to himself.

At exactly five o'clock, the three of them remained the only people in the room. Genevieve, who obviously saw this as a waste of time, took a seat at the table.

Pierre looked imploringly toward Arnold and asked, "May I start, sir?"

"Another couple of minutes please." Mr. Esche was staring blankly at the door to the conference room.

At quarter past five, the door had opened, and Dr. Eicher, who appeared hurried and apprehensive, looked from Arnold to Pierre and spoke, "Mr. Esche, I need to talk to you in private."

Arnold remained still and said calmly, "Erich, I have heard everything. Mr. Libois has explained it all to me. There is no need for further investigation. Please take a seat."

Deciding to go along with Arnold's instruction, the doctor took a seat and once again attempted to corral him, "Mr. Esche, please listen to me. This man needs to be fired along with one of your staff clerks," he explained, pointing at Mr. Libois.

Pierre sat up straight in his seat and looked apprehensively at Arnold Esche.

"There will be no firings while I am still head of this paper. Please, Dr. Eicher, let me explain the situation."

He agreed to remain silent but only until Arnold had spoken. Looking around the room at Arnold, Pierre, and Genevieve, he noticed Archibald was not present.

Finally, as the dust of accusation settled, Arnold began, "I promised the three of you, although Mr. Cunnings is not among us, that I would be giving up my post as president of *The Absolute Watch*. This I will certainly do, and choose a successor I most certainly will. I have asked you to do a bit of research regarding a topic that you would like to discuss, attempting to win my favor . . ."

Pierre stared eagerly at his notes in front of him.

"However, I do not believe that I need to hear them as I have already come to a decision."

The room fell into a spiraling silence. Pierre looked dumbfounded, and the doctor was visibly shocked. Although the doctor did not have his documents with him, he now realized they were useless anyway. Even Genevieve looked horror-struck at the prospect of so much time being wasted on an imaginary witch hunt.

"I have personally chosen Archibald Cunnings as my successor, and when he returns, he will be your boss. I relinquish all my possessions here to him, and I hope you will wish him well once he begins his tenure."

Mr. Libois looked highly upset, although he nodded his head in agreement. Dr. Eicher stood up as politely as he could have made it look and turned to leave the conference room when Arnold called after him, "Please, Erich, I have more to explain."

The doctor returned to his seat, and Arnold continued, "I have just received word, before I had returned from my travels, that I will be a judge in an upcoming hearing for the Board of Governors of The Commerce and Wealth of England."

Pierre was aware of Arnold's political ambition; however, being the only one, he feigned a look of surprise.

"All of you will be attending, as I have reserved seats for you. That includes you, Genevieve."

Although she had been addressed, she looked straight ahead, staring at the wall across from her.

"That settles it. I will see all of you tomorrow at the courthouse."

With this final declaration, Arnold rose from his seat, as did the rest of them, and motioned them out of the room.

Mr. Libois followed Dr. Eicher as both men swept out of the room.

Genevieve stared at Arnold coldly and asked, "Why have you made so many people go through such trouble?" Her voice was icy and spiteful.

Arnold sat back down and answered in a matter-of-fact tone, "I just needed some extra time."

That evening, Arnold had submitted an announcement to the editing department declaring that a public hearing would be held the next day, at the said courthouse, and that it was imperative that all who wished to voice any opinion about his paper should feel welcome to attend.

12

The next morning, Dr. Eicher awoke in his chambers, once again sometime in the afternoon. He had previously asked Francis Thompson to meet him around this time of day so he could escort the doctor to the courthouse for Arnold's impending hearing. He turned over once, almost drifting into slumber, and to his surprise, he saw light breaking through the curtains at his bedside window. He lay there upon the sheets, contemplating whether he should go and humor Arnold's request, for he knew now that all his effort had truly been fruitless. Nevertheless, he concluded that although he would not be the possessor of *The Absolute Watch*, Archibald was certainly a better fit for its pages than Pierre Libois, let alone Arnold Esche, could have ever been.

Not a bad choice at all, he thought to himself.

Perhaps Arnold had given much thought to the paper's direction and surmised that Mr. Cunnings knew the population of Downington better than he or Mr. Libois could have ever hoped to. Settling this score of thought, Dr. Eicher rolled over and clamored out of his comfort.

He went to the lit window and peered out of it. The snow and ice had begun to melt slightly, and indeed the sun in the sky was shining brightly. Rubbing his eyes and turning away from it, he closed the curtain and struggled to find the strength to continue with his awakening. Forcing himself to gather some clothes, he made his way downstairs and into the foyer. Mr. Thompson was waiting for him.

"Sir," his driver began, "I do not mean to rush you, however the time of the hearing is growing ever so near, and we must leave promptly."

"I am ready. Let us go," the doctor muffled lazily.

This hearing was surely to be a waste of some of his time; however, he would at least be in the company of the Board of Governors of The Commerce and Wealth of England, who would surely end whatever the matter promptly in a just manner so that Arnold's decision would be outweighed by them. As he brought about this supposition, the doctor remembered the letter which Archibald Cunnings had given to him before the latter set out on the journey to Siberia. The doctor motioned for Mr. Thompson to wait another moment so he could procure the letter from his desk in the tearoom before they set off once again into the city.

Passing more signs and posters with frivolous phrases and proclamations of its denizens, the doctor closed his eyes as the horse and buggy made its way wobbling down the cobblestone and into the condensed area where the courthouse stood aloft. He was still very tired, and although he attempted to daydream—surely, of the Countess Ms. Freeman—he could not. He began to hear shouts and yells for what seemed like miles. Bothered by the noise and banter outside of the conveyance, he opened his eyes, peeked out of the curtained window, and to his astonishment met the stinging glares of hundreds of people lined along the streets.

This mass of individuals stretched all along the route to the courthouse, and Dr. Eicher was beginning to wonder if he would even make it inside to hear the verdict. As Mr. Thompson pulled to the front of the double white doors, he bade the doctor adieu and promised that he would park near the entrance and await his return, even though the crowd was now heavily swarming the area.

Making his way through the dense procession of bodies, a few guards who held rifles in their arms stopped him and asked what his business was upon entering the building. After explaining his purpose, and most importantly giving his name, they allowed him to slip past the doors and into the entrance hall.

The silence inside was even more deafening than the screams outside. It appeared that not a single person had arrived yet and that the doctor was the only living being inside its walls. He faltered for a moment on the prospect of sitting in on this supposed encounter with Arnold, until he saw a sign at the top of a hallway that read, "Central

Courtroom" and decided that, as a matter of the highest importance which would be decided by the Board of Governors of The Commerce and Wealth of England, this would be the location of their gathering. The same eerie silence followed the doctor all the way down the length of the corridor until he saw two large wooden doors that had plaques upon them. In gold lettering, they bore the title "Board of Governors of The Commerce and Wealth of England" upon them engraved into a black mold.

Drawing breath, the doctor reached for the doors' handles and turned. A burst of conversation met his ears as he stepped into the large, semicircle floor plan of the room. He met high ceilings and drapes of purple silk as he began to take in his surroundings. He noticed a group of gentlemen to his left who were standing and chatting in good spirit. He looked to his right to see a family of about ten—the mother attempting to wrangle her children in their seats while the father stood apprehensively, awaiting the judging of the matter at hand.

As Dr. Eicher made his way down to the front portion of the seating, he saw a couple embracing each other longingly as though they had not seen each other for an eternity. A few rows down to the right, there was a group of lavishly dressed women who looked as though they hadn't seen anyone of lesser stature in their lives. Curiously, the doctor noticed, everyone in the courtroom was holding on to a yellow piece of paper that he had certainly seen before—though he could not quite put his finger on where he had seen it. He then realized that many of the crowd were scribbling notes upon the pamphlet while moving their heads about and eyeing neighboring faces surreptitiously.

The doctor then spotted Mr. Pierre Libois and Ms. Genevieve Allman at the head of the wooden benches sitting generously apart from each other. Deciding that this was the place where he was to sit, it came of no surprise to him that a seat had been reserved for him with his name upon it, directly between his two coworkers. As if they hadn't already affirmed their distaste for each other by their length of distance, Dr. Eicher noticed that Mr. Libois and Ms. Allman both wore an expression of coldness upon their faces. Surely, they would have been talking about the past few days' events and broken into a row about it. He decided the best course of action was to remain silent and not to engage either of them in conversation. The doctor noted that Archibald, again, was missing from their ranks as he surely had not yet returned from his trip from the East.

The three of them, directly seated in front of the judges' bench and just before the floor of speech, sat in silence as countless others continued their conversations and expressions. As he sat observing the room, for there was nothing to speak of to anyone, he turned to his right and saw Henry sitting alone and staring down at his hands, which were laced together in his lap.

As he was removing himself from his seat, attempting to break free of his sitting place and away from Mr. Cunnings and Ms. Allman to speak with Henry, a universal pause fell over all the witnesses as the Board of Governors of The Commerce and Wealth of England appeared from their deliberation room just behind the left of their bench.

A bustling of feet and a thudding of wood followed as the crowd made their way back to their initial places of collectiveness. The seven individuals, including Arnold— all of them sporting long, black cloaks—upon the bench proceeded one by one down to the equal number of chairs that had been laid out before them in unison. Soon there stood four men and three women, hands upon the backs of their chairs, looking seriously out into the gathering.

The first governor spoke, "Ladies and gentlemen, we are pleased to have you all here to bear witness to a testimony of public inquiry. We are all here today on behalf of a young man who wishes to request a plea of termination. He will present his case with utmost honesty and conviction, and we will match this under the pretense of law and how we see fit to enable it in this situation. We ask you, citizens of the court, to show respect and impartialness to his evidence so that all of us upon this bench may be unwavering in our verdict."

With the end of this announcement, the seven judges sat down.

Once again, the first governor spoke, "Please, Henry, you now have the floor of speech."

For the first time since Dr. Eicher had seen him, the youth lifted his head and stood up straight, removing his hands from their locked position and placing one of them behind his back. He opened the gate from the gallery to the floor of speech and turned to face the crowd, standing directly in front of Dr. Eicher, Mr. Libois, and Ms. Allman.

He remained silent for a moment to gather his thoughts and then began, "Fellow humans, I would like to announce a simple change to the judge's words. I now identify myself with a different name. I would like to be addressed henceforth as Henrietta. I now thank you with great sincerity that you are present here today. Even if you are, even now, not listening to a word I am saying, I am nonetheless comforted that you are sitting here before me. I am nervous beyond the highest belief, however I can steady my words, finding solace and strength in your presence.

"You and I share many similarities. Some which I am ashamed to mention, although they bind us ever so closely together. What I mean to say is that I am not with you, and certainly not against you! But I am you. This is undeniable, and if you may understand this point of reference, then it is you who is also standing here talking to yourselves, from within yourselves. The judges before me have asked to plead my case in earnest and with the greatest care of honesty. This I will certainly do, although the most honest man in the world has but one lie to tell. I will not reveal to you my true reason for asking to leave this earth, however I can only ask you to personally imagine your greatest insecurity, and then you will have the clearest picture of my predicament. This quandary is something, again, we all share as *Homo sapiens*.

"At this point in my life, I have become incessantly tired. Though I am quite youthful and full of life, it is doing nothing but prolonging the end to which I am so eagerly ready to obtain. 'Why then is he going through the trouble of presenting this to you and not apprehending his ends by his own means?' you may ask. The answer is as simple as this. If I, in my selfish and most desperate desire, take my own life and leave existence on my own terms, what would you all think of me then? Someone who is not capable of human interaction? Someone who has given way to melancholy and infinite sadness? At these questions, you may only wonder, and wonder will not give you a definite answer, let alone a proper view of which to come so foolishly to one of these conclusions.

"But please ponder this: death is certain, death is inevitable, and death is organic. It is the end goal of life! If one has indeed lived their life to the fullest, are they not now ready to perish? Of course they are! I am not coercing any of you now to ask yourselves if you are ready to move on to whatever meets us at our end. I am asking you to suppose that you, as well as I, have accomplished at this very moment, believed that you understood every single possibility that could occur in one lifetime. Think of your experiences with trial and error, and attempt to decipher an instance where you knew something was going to happen because of a particular action you had carried out. To say, 'What has happened?' and 'What will happen again?' is a pattern that can be followed throughout one's daily operations. This can produce such a mundane and macabre outcome because life is the most detrimental situation a person can experience. When I myself am feeling any type of discomfort paired with intangible pressures, I know full well that I am immersed in the most fruitful and flowering stages of life. I am hyperaware of it, for growth is a tool to be used in private and in secrecy. It is not to be shared in the company of others! However, when a group of individuals is engaged in the lusting actions of laughter and jest, there can be nothing to gain from it.

"Perhaps some are emptying those personal failures and self-doubts onto the plates of others to relieve and put to bed their despair. However, this is not sustenance for another, and no man is wiser from another's woes. If I have any advice to give to you all now, it is that we must respect and take harsh consideration in interacting with others because, as I have previously stated, we are them and they are us. By lashing out upon them and driving their good spirit and nature to the point of desolation, we are merely bringing that back upon ourselves. This brings me to the topic of objectivity that I am so eager to discuss.

"We, as a society, have many real-world activations in place, such as the law that I am attempting to evade before you, because reality is a concept one must grasp from the trauma that we experience. You do not have to accept this notion, but for heaven's sake, you must realize it exists! If you ignore this fact of your senses—sight, hearing, taste, smell, and touch—you are no more alive than you are perceived to be dead to the world. These instincts are essential to us all. Upon focusing these objective impulses, we are but the same as the lesser life-forms that grace this planet so effortlessly. These animals and insects rightfully have no concept of sin because their conscious does not burden them so heavily. Obtaining the distinctions of this objectivity, distancing it from the subjectivity I have a moment ago described, is what makes us human. The ever-looming question is therefore asked: 'Are we but humans or animals?'

"The conclusion that one may come to would be to pick 'either . . . or,' however you cannot choose but one. You must accept both! When an individual can comprehend the differences and similarities of these two notions, then they are free to choose between them when enabling a particular plan of action. This is an extremely powerful and dangerous conclusion to come to. In the objective sense, strictly speaking, we must not think upon action as much as we must simply do it. Metacognition produces nothing but the opposite of reality. Again, ignoring this objective realism will only hurt oneself. However, making the case for the subjective, once an action has occurred, having not dwelled upon it, an individual is free to wonder at the possibilities of that action again. Here, there can be a tug-of-war between one's conscious as to whether they should attempt this action again, understanding the possibility of its outcome, resulting in either following the conscious to not act in that manner again, or realizing that they should not brood upon it and mindlessly carry it out, ignoring the fact that they thought about not doing it in the first place.

"This brings me to the judges that you see behind me, listening ever so intently—I hope—to every word that is erupting from my person. These seven individuals will ultimately decide my fate. This is an objective reality that I understand fully myself. It is their duty to weigh and measure my testimony in a way that gives an agreeable perspective on both of our wants. They want to be just and fair, and I wish to die. I am almost guaranteeing that an outcome can be produced to assure both of us that we can coexist in our ideas. First, as a matter of law, they do not wish to be the guilty party, for then they will not be just and fair. I also wish not to be on the wrong side of the decision, for then I will be forced to continue this existence. I know none of them will allow me to die at their own hands because they do not want blood on them!"

Henry turned for the first time to face the judges, and they all nodded in agreement with him at this supposition.

He continued, "I also will not take my own life, for I do not believe that is a proper method of conveyance from this life to the next. How then will we come to terms of endearment that will satisfy us all? I propose this.

"From a prison of their choice, they will allow a man previously convicted of murder to pull a lever that will drop a grossly heavy object upon me, resulting in my death. Here, a man who is already guilty in terms of law cannot be guilty of this crime twice. You may then ask, 'But how will this suffice in the ignorance of the man pulling the lever? Especially if he is attempting to repent from his previous crime?' First, rest assured, this ignorance will be bliss to him, and this unknown action will never haunt him. Second, pending on the behavior and serious reformation of the individual, there are hundreds of choices—for this I am sure, for there are hundreds of proven murderers. He will be given parole on his first crime to think that he is being released on good terms. I have personally read about cases of murder. Lesser charges than life have been given to a person who has indeed committed the said crime, even if the sentence given in years would surpass the individual's life span. This will allow these judges to make an equal exchange of pass on his life and my own, resulting in a balance of new life and imminent death.

"As for any obstructions of the justice between these judges and myself, if any one of you should feel the need to speak against my wishes and save my life, please do so now so I may explain any of my arguments further."

Dr. Eicher, who was listening just as closely as the judges had done, drew his attention away from Henry and looked about the room. To his surprise, not many of those in the courtroom seemed to be listening at all. Most of them were still scribbling upon the piece of paper in their laps or whispering quietly with those by whom they were accompanied. The doctor spun himself back around and met Henry's eyes. They were welling up as they had done before in their previous meetings.

Wanting to cut across him and attempt to convince the youth otherwise, he noticed Arnold in the far-right corner stand up.

"Young man," Arnold called from the bench, "you cannot seriously believe that we would go through with your request. All people of Downington and its surrounding areas rely on the labor of adept adults to forward our security and prosperity. Surely, you do not think that we would waste your labor as such?"

Now that Arnold began to speak, the attention of the gallery was turned upon him, and there were yells of agreeance at his words, although they were interpreted falsely.

Just then, after he had spoken his piece, one woman from the crowd shouted, "Nay to Arnold Esche!"

A flow of chatter broke out, and now the rumblings in the crowd became louder and louder.

"Order, order please!" exclaimed the second governor.

The kerfuffle began to quell as the third governor proclaimed, "I believe that Mr. Esche is correct in his statement. Young man, although I attempted to understand your point of view, I am not sure that I am ready to believe you a dead man. Your incoherent rambling has not convinced me or any of the others that you deserve to perish."

Dr. Eicher noticed the youth had hung his head shamefully.

Not to be deterred, Henry steadied himself and began, "Your Honor, I . . ."

Within an instant, it seemed as though the youth had trouble breathing. He began to clench his chest as it expanded, grasping for air. Not immediately alarmed, the doctor thought for a moment that Henry was searching for something he had dropped on the floor because he had fallen to one knee and clamored about it with his free hand. The next instant, the youth's other knee had met the ground; he was still clutching his chest, followed by a moment of violent exasperation as he keeled over on his right side and lay faceup, his hand resting upon his heart.

When the doctor sensed no movement, he got up and made his way into the floor of speech from the gallery, grabbing Henry's wrist to check his pulse. The youth had gotten his wish, for now there was no sign of life within him. When the judges had removed themselves from their seats, making screeching noises as they did, the commotion began.

The gallery was now focused on the floor of speech where Henry lay, Dr. Eicher next to him, trying to process what happened. Mr. Libois, who had been eyeing his own yellow paper, looked in astonishment when he tore his vision from it to see the body lying on the ground. Ms. Allman was staring up at Arnold with malicious intent and immediately took to the doctor's side to help him carry the youth out of sight; the gallery could be heard in a deafening roar as they made their way into the judges' deliberation room.

Dr. Eicher and Genevieve Allman carried Henry's hands and feet respectively and laid him on the table at the center of the room. At that moment, all seven judges entered and were in a state of disbelief.

"What the hell just happened?" questioned the fifth governor.

"I am sure the boy was just burnt out and fell to unconsciousness from exhaustion," replied the sixth governor.

When Dr. Eicher explained to them that the youth was gone, they all went to check his pulse as if he were misleading them in his statement.

"My goodness," breathed the first governor. "I suppose it was a heart attack. What else could it have been?"

None of the others spoke, and they all turned to Henry as though he had suddenly moved again. Realizing there was absolutely nothing they could do for him, the governors agreed to call the mortuary so the body could be removed. Only the first governor remained behind along with Dr. Eicher, Ms. Allman, and Mr. Esche—who was moving about the room reading excerpts on the wall about common law, looking as though nothing out of the ordinary had happened.

Genevieve was glaring at him. Dr. Eicher put his hands in his pockets, as to conclude the matter was finally over, and he felt the piece of paper tied up in string that Archibald had given to him. He fingered it in his pocket for a moment, thinking this was certainly not the time to present it; however, it emerged from his jacket, and he turned to give it to the first governor.

"This is from Archibald Cunnings, the new president of *The Absolute Watch*. He requested that I hand it directly to you," the doctor explained, showing it to the governor. "Please take it."

Thinking along the same lines as the doctor about what just happened, the Honorable ultimately decided on distracting himself with it and pulled apart the string and opened the letter.

It read:

> Dear members of the Board of Governors of
> The Commerce and Wealth of England,
> Please accept this declaration in my absence
> that I am handing over all proceedings of *The
> Absolute Watch* to the next available successor.

I am sure Arnold already finalized the paperwork; however, I am hoping that you will amend it and have it signed by its proper adjunct.

Thank you,

Archibald Cunnings

"Arnold," the governor called as he had finished the letter. "Who is this man who claims to have facilitated the handing over of your business?"

Snapping out of his stroll about the room, Arnold came forward in front of the three of them and took the letter to read it over.

"Oh, Mr. Cunnings? He was supposed to fill in for me at *The Absolute Watch*, however it seems that he is no longer willing to do so." He spoke with utter nonchalance.

Dumbfounded, Dr. Eicher and Ms. Allman both requested to read the letter.

After both had scanned it, Arnold announced, "Ah yes, I have not told you that the paper has been sold to a friend of mine. I was just going to have Archibald facilitate the change of hands so its new owner would understand its audience and culture a bit more. I suppose now I can ask this of Dr. Eicher."

He turned to look at the doctor, but in protest, the latter shook his head vigorously. Clearly, this constant morphing of events was taking its toll on him now more than ever.

"It is of no concern to me . . ." The doctor lauded his own indifference.

"Then I will be more than happy to tell Mr. Libois that he will be taking up the post. Genevieve, will you please tell Pierre that I ask this of him?" He ignored the obvious fact that Ms. Allman loathed him and perhaps wished it was him that lay upon the table instead of Henry.

She stormed out of the deliberation chamber, and Arnold went shortly after her.

The doctor, now alone with the first governor in the room, asked the latter, "What would the final verdict have been? All arguments aside, of course."

The governor did not have to think on this very much because he replied immediately, "Does it really matter now? It seems that fate has decided for us."

As she made her way into the flooded street, still buzzing with the talk of what had happened inside the courtroom, for not everyone had been present, Ms. Genevieve Allman had just arrived at her carriage when Mr. Arnold Esche caught up with her. Before she could close the door on the conveyance, Mr. Esche put out a hand to stop it from shutting.

"I am sorry," he blurted out.

Going against her better judgment, she retorted, "Sorry? And what could you possibly be sorry for, per se?

Sorry to me that you ruined the lives of countless others, not to mention my own most of all? I know how selfish of a person you are, and no words or actions at this point could ever change my perception of you. I hate you!"

"I understand. However, a great capacity for loathing is not possible without a great capacity for affection. You and your mother are so very much alike."

Genevieve started for a moment and then paused. She then claimed, "You never even knew her! I didn't even know her."

"On the contrary, I knew her very well unlike yourself. Florence was quite the Quintrell as I know you to be. So full of life and prowess and she was very much aware of it. I was there the night on which I believed you to be conceived, ironically enough. Your father was in a drunken stupor, and your mother was playing the poor man as if he were an entertainer producing his most choreographed talents for her to witness."

"What are you talking about?" she was berating him as if he were a madman.

"I care for you in such a way you could not understand. You will never understand because it is bad for business, and that is the only relationship we have ever known!"

She pushed him away from the carriage and slammed the door. Asking the driver to make haste, she left him in his own small circle within the crowd to find his way back to the courthouse.

As he returned to the double white doors of the courthouse, feeling as though he had spoken his piece, Arnold Esche spotted Dr. Eicher coming down the corridor from where the entrance to the main courtroom had been, alone.

He strode up to him, but the doctor was in no mood to speak.

"Please, Erich," he asked him in earnest, "will you please be the one to tell Mr. Libois that he is to take up Mr. Cunnings's vacant post?"

Clearly discombobulated, the doctor hesitantly agreed so that he could pass Mr. Esche and be on his way home. Thanking him, Mr. Esche followed Dr. Eicher back out of the front doors of the courthouse where they unceremoniously parted ways.

Finding Francis Thompson in his mode of transport quite easily, for now the mass of individuals was beginning to disperse, Dr. Eicher let out a long sigh of relief at the sight of him.

"I heard screams and laughter as everyone came out of the courthouse. What has happened?"

"Francis, I will explain when we arrive back at my residence. I need some quiet now, if you please."

13

Back at her late father's residence, Genevieve Allman was nestled alone, lying with her head upon her arms. She was awfully exhausted from the spectacle of the trial she had witnessed, coupled with Arnold's absurd revelation that he had been familiar with the former's mother. A single candle lay burning upon the wooden table that sat in the middle of the room, her father's possessions now neatly arranged in the same lonely corner. Although she was very tired, she could not seem to pry herself away from the structure and retire to bed because her mind was working furiously. What had happened to that boy that made him perish in such a horribly abrupt manner? She understood that he must've been overwhelmed at the sight of so many people gathered around him, although that would simply make an individual faint, not die.

She began to reflect on these spectators that were moments before gathered in the courthouse. It reminded her of those who were employed at *The Absolute Watch*. Hundreds of faces that needed assistance. Those seemingly powerless to affect any sort of outcome all gathered to become involved in something bigger than themselves. Who then, in their right mind, would deprive them of such an achievement? Arnold, of course. Mr. Esche who only cared for himself. Mr. Arnold Esche who stood alone in striking down whatever the youth had attempted to win, whatever was dear to him. How could one, just one, person become so self-absorbed and so self-centered that everything must revolve around him?

She picked up her head from the table and looked to the burning wax that was now at half-life. It was pitch-black outside. The glow of the enflamed wick cast a yellowish radiance against Genevieve's skin, and her shadow was plastered upon the wall in the same shade as the picturesque darkness that was visible through the windows. Just then, as she thought now was the time to turn in, for her eyelids were beginning to droop, she heard a polite rapping on the front door of the house.

Thinking this was probably Arnold's feeble attempt to apologize, she got up and was not surprised when she reached the door, opened it, and saw the figure of a man just beyond the doorway. As he stepped into the dim light that emerged from behind her, Genevieve noticed that it was not Mr. Esche but a man of similar stature and dress.

Not recognizing him, she asked in a curious manner, "To whom do I owe this late-night arrival?"

The man gave a deep bow and announced, "It is I, Genevieve. Robert Allagash."

Needing a moment to mull over this reply, her eyes became wide and awake at the realization that this was the boy she had known so very long ago when she was just a child.

"Robert? Could it really be you?"

"It is indeed. Please forgive me for passing so late upon your doorstep, but I felt that I must seek you out, for I had failed to do so on the first occasion."

Not understanding what Robert had meant by "the first occasion," she led him inside, and both sat down at the table. Genevieve took the place where she had been a minute before.

"First, I'd just like to say that I cannot believe that you are here! I would have thought that a man in your position would be a great traveler of the world."

He gave a small chuckle. "Yes, I have accomplished many of the feats you would have believed me to engage in. I have quite frankly been to many places and foreign lands, but I have not found comfort or feelings of admiration anywhere quite as strong as in Downington in which I now reside. I am an accomplished medical doctor, and my practice is located just adjacent to the city."

She began fantasizing about his wide range of fanciful patients and for those whom he would care.

"However, I have not come here tonight to discuss myself," he began. "I am here in your presence because, as I have said, the first time I wanted to reintroduce myself, I had not been successful. I came across an article in *The Absolute Watch* about nationalism, and I simply fell in love with it. I found it prominent to seek out its author to congratulate him on his splendid ideas. When I arrived at his headquarters, there stood a massive, shifting attendance. I was in awe as to how many people must've felt the same as I, and I attempted to wade through them as to make my way to the front. A few clashes broke out, and I became overwhelmed in the sea of individuals.

"A man came out of the topmost window and seemed to calm everyone down, and that was when I laid my eyes upon you. I knew it had to be you because your face has scarcely changed since I last remember placing my gaze upon it. When the murmurs and jostling had ceased enough for me to approach, you had turned and gone inside its doors. At that moment, I admit, I lost my stomach for approaching you, and I left, vowing to see you again.

"I found my next chance this evening as I was outside of the courthouse. Again, the man who had written the article about our country alerted his supporters in a new piece of writing welcoming them to attend tonight's proceedings. I did so, and there again you were! I saw you arrive, although I could not physically get to you as the courtroom had been announced full and there were, again, hundreds of others packed along the streets. When you left, another man had already been following you, and I had assumed him your significant other. Disheartened, I meekly watched you speak with him.

"But to my surprise—and luck, so I thought—you had slammed the door in his face and began trotting off. I took the opportunity now given to me to follow you in my own conveyance, and here I am before you! I am sorry that I had not immediately caught your attention, for I was gathering up the courage to place a knock upon your door." He finished in fatigue.

Genevieve was staring at him blankly, amassing all his words for herself to interpret. This man was certainly not the Robert Allagash she remembered as a youth. He was impishly shy, and not to mention, he was a fan of Arnold's! She thought it best to ask him his true intentions before she began judging him further.

"Please, in earnest, tell me what your true purpose in coming to meet me was."

Mr. Allagash looked so excited that he was about to explode. He attempted to calm himself before asking outright, "I wanted to ask for your hand in marriage."

As these words left his mouth, he seemed at least for a moment to settle down, although his apprehension was still apparent on his face.

Genevieve's expression became sour. This man with whom she had no contact for years, only knowing him as a child, was asking her to be swept away immediately? Could he have proposed anything on lesser grounds? She had heard quite enough.

She tried to be as courteous as she could allow herself to be and replied, "I decline. And if you please, I am very tired. I would very much like to be left alone to retire as it is getting late."

At this answer, Robert Allagash's expression became equally as displeased. He stood up, knocking the chair over behind him, and bellowed, "Fine. Enjoy your excuse of a dwelling and a life of being equally as insignificant!" He turned on his heel and slammed the door shut as he made his way through the threshold.

The chattering of wheels followed as Genevieve's childhood acquaintance left her in the silence she so desired at that moment.

What a weak and idiotic man he has grown to become.

Still fuming, she strode over to her father's remnants and placed them crate by crate outside in the back of the house. She then went inside and removed the quarter stick of light from the table, returning once again to the structure's rear. Looking upon what was left of her father, she had no regret as she tossed the candle into the innumerable papers, memos, and utensils. After a moment's ignition, all of it went up in flames.

Further into the night, Arnold Esche was sitting alone in the conference room at *The Absolute Watch*. He was catching up on past editions of the paper that had been published in his absence; he grinned broadly at the edition in which his second piece of writing appeared. Thinking to himself that every course of action he had previously taken was now leading up to their apex, he sat back and drank in the four walls with which he would soon be unfamiliar. Arnold had made it official. The rights of *The Absolute Watch*, through the Board of Governors of The Commerce and Wealth of England, had been sold. This building was to be demolished, and the land would be usurped by the same governing body that approved the said paperwork. Arnold was satisfied.

However, his work was not yet complete. He replaced the now puddles of wax with brand-new candles and used the old sparks to ignite the new. A weak attempt to alert the party inside that someone was at the entrance hit Arnold's ears faintly.

"Please come in," he assured its identity.

Archibald Cunnings, looking worn out and apprehensive, was now in this room for the first time in two weeks. His round spectacles were shining in the fresh radiance of the light.

"I have done what you have asked of me," he admitted, addressing Arnold. "Here is your medal."

He handed Mr. Esche the bronze box, and the latter opened it just as the former had when he reached Siberia.

"Excellent!" Arnold exclaimed. He pinned the silver medal to his breast, and his face lit up brighter than the candles before him.

Clearly not as enthusiastic, Archibald gave a faint smile.

Mr. Esche spoke directly to him, "Mr. Cunnings, I thank you greatly for your dedication. On top of this recognition, I would also like to speak to you on the matter of your letter to the Board of Governors of The Commerce and Wealth of England."

Archibald looked nervously in Mr. Esche's direction.

"Please do not think I am upset," he began. "I had almost expected this from you. That journey certainly would have taken much out of you. It takes a particular kind of person to run such a commodity as a paper."

Archibald noticed the tone in Arnold's voice meant that the latter was speaking about himself.

"This is why I have appointed a friend from the region to which you have just traveled. He is more than capable of understanding the delicate balance of powers that be about media and propaganda. The operation that he ran formerly has given me this confidence. For him to agree, I had to do him but a small favor." Arnold motioned to the decoration on the left side of his chest.

Archibald followed these words carefully, and then he began to form their supposed meaning. The train ride to the Far East, the rich passengers, Georgy, the prisoners in the rear car, the man in military uniform.

"But, Mr. Esche! How could you do something so conniving?" Archibald pleaded in horror.

"My dear fellow! This operation was nothing of the sort! All were in agreeance and had accepted the terms and conditions. Many were just ignorant of the outcome."

Arnold stood up from the head of the conference table and made his way over to Archibald and placed both hands on the latter's shoulders.

"Do you not see that objective goals possess subjective outcomes? Have you not noticed that in all these years, I have worked on propelling the paper's image that I have made it impenetrable by outside forces? The only way to further this cause was to hand it to an outside force itself! This way, my next move would not be affected by it. If I were still in charge of *The Absolute Watch* as I ran a political campaign, do you think that others would have let me fill a position? Of course not! There would have been too much noticeable influence!"

Archibald contemplated Arnold's words, and although he understood his actions, he refused to believe or accept its processes.

"Now more than ever," Mr. Esche assured Mr. Cunnings, "I need your help. Please assist me one more time as I ask you to head my push for office. I trust you, and I promise that if I succeed, your loyalty will not be in vain."

Thinking painfully of Georgy, Archibald surmised that to be in a position of secondary power was much greater than carrying out the heaviest burden in the top position. Mr. Cunnings drew a great breath and agreed to assist his twice-appointed boss.

"Splendid."

Mr. Esche left the room momentarily to fetch two highball glasses and a container of whiskey and poured two drinks. He raised his for a toast, and Archibald did the same.

"To the future and all of its prosperities!"

They both downed their potion.

"Now, if you please, Archibald, I would like some time to myself for the rest of the evening to write some letters."

Agreeing that they would both meet tomorrow in the same place, Archibald Cunnings bowed out with mechanical motion and left Arnold once again as the sole individual in the conference room.

Mr. Esche picked up a quill and two pieces of parchment. On the first he wrote:

Dear Pierre,

I congratulate you on your new position as chieftain of affairs at *The Absolute Watch*.

You are to be stationed in Siberia, a first-class train ticket will be purchased on your behalf, and you will leave in expediency. I hope that you will carry out your duties as efficiently as I am sure you are capable of. You will face many hardships in your tenure, but fear not because there are others you may align yourself with that will help you achieve success. Speaking of which, I advise you to take my former staff clerk, Sebastian, with you, as he has already seemed to serve you well in my absence. Arrangements can certainly be made for him as well if you decide to honor this piece of advice. If you need to call upon me for anything, please do not hesitate, for my communication channels will be free from obstruction at your new post. Although I admit you were not my first choice for this role, please do not let that hinder the fact that you are now the one appointed. From here on out, we may be able to continue the good name and prosperity *The Absolute Watch* has bestowed upon both of us.

Best regards,

Arnold Esche

After finishing this first proclamation to Pierre Libois, Arnold picked up the second piece of parchment, thought for a moment, then began:

Dear Sergey Mikhailovich,

Well done! Events could not have happened in such favor as ours have. I am glad that you have accepted the sale of my business with open arms. I was more than happy to send workers your way at your request, for I have had many at my disposal. Could we have struck a better deal? I think not! Hopefully, when we are both so soundly established, our collusion can produce a trust and friendship the likes of which the world has never seen before! Both of our countries are truly great and have the highest understanding of human nature possible. With this ideal in mind, we can bridge any gap that comes between us. I understand that you are very busy, however when we both have ample time and my victory has come to pass, we may be able to meet and further discuss our proposals for the future of our respective nations. Hoping to hear back from you soon.

Your veritable counterpart,

Arnold Esche

In the afternoon that followed, Erich Eicher awoke at midday to more pleasant weather. The temperature was warmer, and the sun was once again shining through his window, making the inside of his lids glow as he awoke without opening them. He thought of the past days' events for but a moment as he decided to push them out of his mind. Not having to make great efforts to reach full consciousness, he felt refreshed as he remembered that tonight was his most anticipated event since Joanne Freeman had first come to visit him. He hopped out of his resting place with enthusiasm and put himself together hurriedly, as he would soon have to call for Francis Thompson to meet him.

In a dreamlike state, Dr. Eicher imagined his eventual encounter with Ms. Freeman. They were sharing beverages and gaily engaging in conversation. She would be most enthralled with him as he supposed that they should become a unit. A perfect time and place to reveal this to her.

As he made his way down into the foyer, he noticed that a dinner jacket was hung upon the edge of the door that stood ajar at the entrance to the house. Erich supposed that Mr. Thomson had already arrived, and he had guessed correctly. Sitting patiently in the tearoom was Francis Thompson, hands in his lap, looking about the room, and humming excitedly.

"Doctor," he turned his head to greet him, "the day is finally here. My first formal event, and as you can see, I can hardly contain my anticipation!"

The doctor smiled at him and motioned to Mr. Thompson that they should be on their way. Taking his jacket from the corner of the door, Mr. Thompson slipped it on once more and proceeded to lead Dr. Eicher to their carriage.

As they began to make their way out of the confines of Downington, Dr. Eicher engaged once more in daydreaming while Francis babbled on about none other than Edward Montclair. The stalks of winter wheat on their usual path were shining in the sun, and the sky was a clear, electric blue. Pools of water were formed in scattered spots where the previous snowfall had melted. An hour's journey was not unusual; however, this muddy, sodden landscape hindered them in such a way that it took longer for them to reach Joanne's estate. As they made their way through the countryside, they started to see a greater amount of traffic.

Can all of these conveyances be headed to this particular party?

This thought supposed by both the doctor and Mr. Thompson was answered as they were made to park several yards away from the house on the hill. All the transports were parked neatly on either side of the path, leaving a small strip of land up the middle for them to pass through. There was even a line at the gate protruding from the guard's post, to ask for names of attendees so that they might be properly identified. Dr. Eicher and Francis Thompson removed themselves from their conveyance and made their way to stand in the line of guests.

Mr. Thompson was moving his head around, looking hither and thither as he had in Dr. Eicher's tearoom, although this was of a negative connotation instead of a hopeful one.

"I do believe we were supposed to bring offerings," he said to the doctor.

Many of the ladies and gentlemen present were holding small tokens wrapped in colored paper garnished with trappings.

"We will surely have to admit that we left them behind by mistake," the doctor was now caught in a sense of apprehension as well.

As they waited for the snakelike procession to shorten, Dr. Eicher listened intently to those speaking around him.

"I do hope the old man has something for us in return!" a middle-aged man said imploringly to a group of what seemed to be close friends about him.

"Not likely," returned a woman from the group. "This party is our gift. I assure you, it will not disappoint! Arthur pulls out all of the stops when entertaining."

This gave the doctor a greater stomach for the event to come. Surely, Joanne's father was just as elegant as she and took to seriousness in the affairs of others, especially if they were all to gather at his request. Joanne had mentioned that this gathering was to be business oriented, and what better way to attain others' attentiveness than through a great spectacle?

As they finally made their way past the gate, the guards—giving them a nod and remembering them all the while checking their names—allowed them passage to address the next set of hopefuls. Another guard lay waiting at the front doors, holding them open, and the doctor and Mr. Thompson were once again inside the sitting room of Joanne's estate.

The room was brilliantly lit with the chandeliers draped in emerald green with wall hangings to match. The purple ones that hung there before had obviously been taken down. Over the heads of a few circles of individuals who stood guffawing and speaking loudly in front of them, the doctor could see that the main study was packed with partygoers. As they wondered how they were going to make their way through the dense body, the doctor and Mr. Thompson were approached by Edward Montclair, who spotted them and waved them down. Mr. Thompson's eyes lit up, and he began to blush.

"Good evening, gentlemen," his voice was monotone yet sincere. "Please do help yourself to some hors d'oeuvres." He motioned a butler over to them, and they surveyed the bites interestedly. "Francis, may I have a quick word?"

Feeling as though he must leave the doctor's presence for this, he agreed, and Mr. Montclair led him aside to tell him something. Standing alone, though not far away, the doctor eyed the pair as they exchanged words. After a second or so, Mr. Montclair left Francis to return to Dr. Eicher.

Within a few steps, Francis similarly grabbed the doctor's attention. "Edward has just told me that Joanne is not well."

The doctor experienced a quiet panic.

"She is not physically ill, he tells me, but she just isn't in the right state to entertain anyone right now. Mr. Montclair explained that not even her relation is present."

The doctor thought once again of the past day's events and concluded that Henry's death might have a hand in it. Certainly, Peter was to be distraught, but was Joanne possibly feeling guilty about her dislike for the youth?

"Additionally, Mr. Montclair said he would be back in a moment with Mr. Freeman so as to introduce us."

Understanding that it would be most appropriate for them to meet the organizer, let alone the father of his interest, the doctor agreed, and they awaited Arthur Freeman's arrival.

After a few moments' wait, a bald man with a pointed beard, dressed in the same color as the decorations, approached them.

"Gentlemen!" he bellowed gaily. "Thank you so much on my own behalf for coming." He shook hands with Mr. Thompson first, then Dr. Eicher, pulling both in for an embrace. "You two are familiar with my daughter, are you not?"

Both nodded their heads in acknowledgment.

"Splendid, splendid. Which of you would be Dr. Eicher then?"

Erich Eicher spoke in turn, "I am, sir, and may I say that it is an honor to make your acquaintance."

"I, too, am honored. Would you mind if we had a quick word?"

Not at all against this proposal, the doctor and Mr. Freeman left Mr. Thompson and Mr. Montclair in the sitting area, and the former made their way outside onto the lawn of the grounds off its path.

The doctor spoke first, "This is certainly an extravagant event," not wanting to flatter him so much as to gain his comfort.

"Indeed, it is," Mr. Freeman agreed. "However, if you don't mind, I'd like to speak on something other than the party at the moment."

By this request, the doctor asked him to go on.

"It is my daughter, you see, as you might have guessed. She is not well just now and refuses to come down and mingle with the guests. I am afraid she has gotten the idea in her head that she does not want a hand in my personal affairs."

The doctor already knew of this, as she had revealed it to him previously, but not wanting to interrupt, he put on a face of eagerness to hear more.

"She believes that she is on the cusp of some avant-garde ideas and refuses to realize that my business is of a serious nature. I have no other heir to bequeath and bestow this upon. As a doctor of the mind, please attempt to convince her that it is her duty to accept my wishes. I do not trust anyone but my own blood in this manner. She has spoken of you many times, and she will undoubtedly take your consideration to greater lengths than my own. She thinks very highly of you, and I hope that you can understand my position from an outsider's perspective."

Although this was an incontrovertible excuse to go seek out Joanne alone and spend some time with her, the doctor remembered what Francis had passed on to him from her own personal adjunct. Thinking back and forth in a semicritical state, Dr. Eicher ultimately promised Joanne's father that he would speak to her on the matter.

"Excellent. Please do your best to ease into it, if you will. She can sometimes be quite dramatic in her current state."

As Mr. Freeman led them both back into the sitting room, the two drivers had vanished. Promising the doctor an expensive cigar and aged spirits upon his return, Mr. Freeman disappeared from the area himself, leaving the doctor to venture on his own to the highest room in the estate and solicit an appearance from Joanne.

He climbed the stairs gingerly to balance the feeling of his heavy feet and lightheartedness. He was more than willing to see and speak to her, for she had invited him to this soiree personally, although now he was trying to call to her on someone else's behalf. As he reached her door, he could hear snuffed sobbing. He would not disturb her. He couldn't. He could already tell that Mr. Montclair was steering him in the correct direction. He turned to leave, but as he did, he pictured the face he knew to be hers and was instantly filled with a desire to help her. Not for her father or for anyone else, but to comfort her because he cared so deeply for her.

He knocked softly upon the door, and the tears were instantly quelled.

Joanne called angrily, "Is that you again, Father? Go away! I refuse! I refuse!"

Without a second thought, Dr. Eicher turned the handle on the door, and to his surprise, it was unlocked. He pushed the wooden structure past its frame and saw Joanne, dressed as if she was indeed attending the party, lying facedown on her bed with her head in her hands. She picked up her head and turned around to see the doctor in a state of shock and sallowness.

"Erich! I am so sorry you must see me like this. It is all because of Father. He doesn't understand that I cannot be alone in apprehending his tasks for him. Why does he loathe me so?"

The doctor remained silent but slowly walked to her bedside. He was now the one who was feeling guilty about his presence before her.

"Please, Joanne, rise from your place of sorrow. Your father said he does not trust another. At least hear him out."

"No. I refuse." She laid her head back down on the sheets.

The doctor attempted to bring her around once again. "Perhaps you are not feeling well because of what has happened to Henry yesterday?"

She indeed picked up her head once again but scoffed, "I do not care about him! I am glad that he is dead. Of that, at least, I can be glad that I am rid of him."

The doctor was disheartened to hear this. Could Joanne really have felt such hatred toward a youth attempting only to assist her relation?

"Henry was only trying to help Peter find his way, how can you disdain him for such an honest effort?"

She now sat up and faced the doctor. "All he did was stall Peter's progress! Peter had to grow up sometime, and he could not do that with someone whispering in his ear about freedom and lethargy while the world around him was advancing ever so rapidly."

The doctor did not know where his next words came from. Perhaps it was because he thought he truly wanted to understand the subsequent error of her ways, or perhaps he wanted her to see things from a similar perspective. But he let out, "Perhaps you are so spiteful of Henry because he lives the life you could only wish to. Helping others break free from their shell when you could not hope to do the same. You are unable to do so, and that is why you are sitting here alone and wallowing in your own tears. You are blaming your father the same way you are blaming Henry for holding someone back."

This obviously did not have the effect the doctor wished because, instantly, Johnna became a shade of red that put her flamingo walls to shame.

She sobbed even harder than before and breathed, "How could you defend these two when clearly it is I who is in desperate need of recovery? Me! I took your advice and attempted to explain to Father that all his talk was nonsense. He not only laughed but disowned me. It is your fault that I am in such a predicament. I should have just fled from all of this without a word, yet here I am further explaining myself." She approached him quickly.

He wanted to close in around her. Squeeze the anxiety from her. Take all the stabbings away that she was experiencing. Ironically, the doctor himself felt something like this pass through him, and he was at a loss until his nerves had brought him to the area of impact upon his left side. His arm had been struck swiftly. The doctor grimaced intensely. This was opposite the human contact he'd been yearning for. Joanne moved away from him and did not look remorseful, although she understood what she had done. Dr. Eicher could not move. He merely stared her directly in the pupils as to make a photographic memory of them. Without a word, he turned and left her to slam the door behind him as he made his way through the threshold.

Silently, as if he were floating, Dr. Eicher made his way back to a set of stairs that led down to the sitting area. He spotted Mr. Montclair and Mr. Thompson laughing jovially with a group of others and noticed that Mr. Freeman was entering the study with two cigars in his hand, smoking a third, and carrying two unfilled glasses. Dr. Eicher did not remember anything after this. Ignoring the fact that everyone else but he was drinking heavily and dancing unbothered about him, he swept past them all without a notion and made his way back to the conveyance where he was left to await Francis Thompson in his blacked-out disregard.

"That is not at all the problem, my dear. It is just that I have talked with the accounting and human resources managers, and it seems that they will not be hiring another manager to take over production duties. If I remain here, I will be doing twice the work for no more incentive."

She does look quite tired, thought Ms. Allman.

"I came to seek you out to ask you if you would not quit this place as well and join me somewhere else as an assistant?"

Genevieve was shocked to hear this. *But*, she thought momentarily, *an assistant?*

Surely, she was in that position already, and she was doing much more than that for Arnold now.

"I would enjoy your confidence and prowess very much wherever I should go. I just have a bad feeling about this business in the long term. With my résumé as a manager, I should have no trouble being put on elsewhere. What do you say?"

Genevieve thought hard for a length of seconds, but ultimately, she decided that *The Absolute Watch* needed her with Arnold and his cronies around.

"I am sorry, but I will have to decline. This paper needs me."

Understanding her decision, the packaging and production manager shook her hand firmly and said, "I wish you all the best. Please do not hesitate to seek me out in the future."

She turned and left Genevieve standing in the middle of the production floor.

"A bad feeling about this business," she had said. Impossible, thought Ms. Allman. *The reputation of this place alone was in good standing, whether or not Arnold had published that piece of rubbish.*

She made her way back upstairs, thinking that Arnold might finally be awake, and alas, the light was on in his room. She strode over to it, knocked, and stood back as the door swung open.

Mr. Esche smiled as he saw that his young secretary was standing at his residence awaiting his instruction.

"Good morning," he bellowed.

Genevieve merely spluttered, "Do you have my notes for the day?"

"Ah yes," Arnold turned and made his way to his desk. He handed Genevieve one piece of paper that read:

Meeting in the conference room at 17:00.

Feeling as though this were his idea of a joke, she said no more and made her way to the conference room to prepare.

As she made her way into the said room, Pierre was again the sole individual sitting there at its table. He was not reading letters but writing something down, probably for Arnold and the rest to hear. He picked up his head to see Genevieve, and he too gave her a smirk. She ignored him and began rummaging in a box of quills and ink to